SHADOW JUMPER

The Quest

A novel by
Cait Shea

Grosvenor House
Publishing Limited

All rights reserved
Copyright © Cait Shea, 2019

The right of Cait Shea to be identified as the author of this
work has been asserted in accordance with Section 78
of the Copyright, Designs and Patents Act 1988

The book cover is copyright to Cait Shea

This book is published by
Grosvenor House Publishing Ltd
Link House
140 The Broadway, Tolworth, Surrey, KT6 7HT.
www.grosvenorhousepublishing.co.uk

This book is sold subject to the conditions that it shall not, by way of
trade or otherwise, be lent, resold, hired out or otherwise circulated
without the author's or publisher's prior consent in any form of binding or
cover other than that in which it is published and
without a similar condition including this condition being imposed
on the subsequent purchaser.

This book is a work of fiction. Any resemblance to
people or events, past or present, is purely coincidental.

A CIP record for this book
is available from the British Library

ISBN 978-1-78623-579-4

CHAPTER 1
Sinead's Foley

A deafening bang vibrated through the darkness as the church doors burst open. A tall slim girl with long black hair ran barefoot into the night. Sweat fell down her face as she ran down the road leading away from the church, heading towards the beach. Looking over her shoulder as she ran, it was difficult to make out the form that chased her, but she could sense it was close behind. The howling cut through the darkness, as the beast bawled a deep rasping scream, in pursuit of its prey. Its large outstretched wings pulsating as it pushed through the night, swooping up and down, using the wind as its frameless carriage, carrying it swiftly towards the ocean.

The young girl ran along the shoreline, her pink flowery pajamas were damp from the sea spray, her feet frozen on the cold wet sand. She cried out for her parents as she ran shouting, "Mum, dad come back", but there was nothing, no sound not even a whisper. The harder she tried, the more difficult it got to push the words out; tears flowed down her cheeks as she pleaded with silent words for her parents to come and rescue her. She could only see a short distance in front of her, as she squinted her eyes, forcing them to see through the blackness of the night, the sound of the crashing waves came closer. Suddenly she was knee deep in water, and the loud banging noise thudded behind her; the wind picked up, twisting the waves into a funnel, sucking her up into its watery cage. There was no escape; she was trapped.

Sinead Foley sat up in her bed with a jolt, her heart was pounding in her chest and vibrating in her ears. Her pink flowery pajamas were damp, and her hair and face were wet. She sat upright in her bed, shivering from the cold, or was it the dreaded nightmare she had just awoken from that made her body tremble? The bedroom window tossed back as it crashed against the outside of the bedroom wall. The curtains flapped in the wind, and the rain poured through the open window.

The top of Sinead's bed, which sat against the window, was now wet. She jumped up on her bed, leaned out of the window and grabbed at the window latch. A big storm had kicked off during the night; the wind howled, and the rain battered the little house. In the distance, Sinead could hear the waves crash as she pulled the window shut, locking the storm outside.

She sat on her bed; her body shook as a chill took residence in her bones. A damp, wet sensation pushed its way through, pricking her skin and causing bumps to develop underneath. Prickly, painful bumps. The bed was now very wet, and so were Sinead's pajamas. With a deep sigh, she slowly lowered both legs to the floor, treating them as precious, delicate objects. She hated the prickly, painful sensation that ran down both limbs. Shifting her focus from the storm outside, that continued to howl and batter her bedroom window like some angry gargoyle, Sinead picked herself up, put on a new set of pajamas, towel-dried her hair, and got a fresh quilt from her wardrobe. She left the damp bundle of clothes on the floor and headed out of her bedroom and down the hallway. She quietly tip toed towards the second bedroom and gently opened the door. Her gran was sleeping peacefully. Sinead stood by the bedroom door for a few moments as she watched the blankets on her gran's bed gently rise and fall, in motion with her breathing. Sinead turned gently and walked quietly to the stairs and headed to the front room, where she made a fresh bed for herself on the sofa. She slid between the quilt and the sofa cushions; the heat slowly engulfed her feet and pushed its way up like a warm current taking possession of her limbs, pushing out the cold chill that tried to take her bones as a hostage. She could feel herself drift, drift on a current of heat, while the howling storm, that once dominated her sleep, was becoming a distant murmur. The island had always been inflicted by wild storms that cut across the Atlantic Ocean; Sinead's bedroom, being at the back of the house, always caught the brunt of the storm, but now as she snuggled down on the sofa at the front of the house in her gran's living room, she drifted off to sleep. Morning was still a long way off.

The sunlight bled through the curtains, creating an animation of images on the living room floor. Sinead rubbed her eyes and slowly sat up on the sofa. She scanned the room taking in her surroundings; this was not her bedroom. Outside birds chirped, and the ocean crashed on the beach. She could hear the sound of pushing and shoving. Sinead jumped off the sofa and ran to the front door. There she saw her gran rearranging the garden furniture.

"Gran, what are you doing?"

"Oh, sorry did I wake you, love?"

"That's not what I mean, you should have called me."

"It's fine; just a couple of sun loungers. I can manage that much on my own."

Sinead helped her gran pick up the last chair and leant it against the wall under the bay window.

"No one would ever think we had a storm last night," her gran said, looking around, taking in the scenery of the beautiful spring morning. "Let's go inside and I'll fix us some breakfast. I've also got some news for you?"

"News? What News?"

But her gran was *already* walking into the house.

"Gran, Gran what news?" Sinead ran after her.

"Would you like some bacon and eggs, love?" Gran said as she turned the cooker on and rested the frying pan on top.

"Yes, that sounds lovely," Sinead said, and her tummy rumbled in agreement.

"So, this news you have for me?" Sinead tried to sound casual as she started to set the table for breakfast. Patience wasn't her strong suit, but she knew her gran would tell her when she was ready.

"I got a call from your aunty in New York," her gran said, as she adjusted the heat on the cooker, and then flicked over the eggs in the frying pan. Remember little Elicia? She is making her first communion in a couple of months."

"Oh wow, really?" Sinead tried to sound a little enthusiastic as she poured them both a cup of tea, but if that was Gran's great news, Sinead had already lost interest.

"I might go down to the beach after breakfast, and I can walk by the shops if you need anything," Sinead said, as she moved on from the whole church conversation, and avoiding the importance of God and prayer that was most likely to follow. If she got to the beach early, she could have a little hunt and see what the storm had washed up during the night.

"Yes, we do need some more milk and eggs," her gran said as she placed a cooked breakfast in front of Sinead. "But like I was saying, your aunty phoned," her gran repeating what she had said. Gran's do that, repeat themselves; "I guess it comes with old age", Sinead thought, as she cut a piece of bacon.

"So, we have been invited to New York, in May, for a couple of weeks," her gran paused and looked at Sinead who was now turning red and burst into a fit of coughing.

"Oh dear, are you ok?"

Sinead nodded a yes as she slugged down some tea. "Yes, I think my food went down the wrong pipe," she gasped "are we really going to New York?"

"Yes, we are," Gran smiled.

"Oh my gosh, Gran, that's great news!" Sinead jumped up, ran to the other end of the table and hugged her Gran. "I can't believe it; we are actually going."

"Yes, we are certainly going," said gran as she hugged her granddaughter and quietly thought that this could also be a lovely way to celebrate Sinead's 13th birthday.

After breakfast, Sinead walked down the road towards the beach; in the distance she could see the fishing boats bobbing up and down as they sailed out onto the big blue ocean. Their hearts set on returning with a full catch for the day. Sinead looked past the boats, over the ocean, and onto the horizon, where the sea appeared to meet the sky, and beyond that invisible line was New York City. Soon she would be there, walking down the streets, looking at the fashion in the windows of some of the most famous shops in the world. Oh, but they don't call them shops in New York; there they are called stores. She would visit all the famous stores, Sinead promised herself. As she allowed her thoughts to leave the island and whisk her off to the Big Apple, where she could disappear into a sea of people and nobody would know who she was. There, she could be Sinead Foley, the famous fashion designer, who was in town for the fashion week, and she would casually rub shoulders with other designers.

"Morning, Sinead." A male voice startled her as it cut into her dream, and with a jump she was back on the island.

"Sorry, didn't mean to make you jump," the man said, apologetically.

"Oh, you didn't, Father Brian," she said trying to hide any tremor in her voice, as the casually dressed man in a dark blue, cable-knit roll-neck, blue denim jeans, and black brogues walked next to her.

"It looks like it's going to be a lovely day," he nodded towards the sun in the sky, shining down on the island and on the peaceful ocean. "Apparently there was a tornado out at sea last night."

'Oh really?" Sinead said surprised and curious.

"Apparently so," Father Brian repeated, not mentioning where he had got his information from. "And how is your gran?"

"She's well, thank you Father."

"Well I guess you're heading to the beach to do a bit of scavenger hunting, so I won't hold you up," he said. "See you and your gran at church tomorrow," he said, as he picked up his pace and turned right to walk up Church Road, that led to the little church on the hill, which overlooked the ocean.

"Goodbye Father," Sinead responded, as she carried on walking down the Beach Road, which in fact led straight to the harbour, where a small walkway called The Boreen cut off from the road and led down to the beach.

Sinead liked Father Brian; he seemed to understand young people, but she didn't see why she had to call him father - he wasn't her father; he wasn't anyone's father. God had a weird way of doing things; he would take her own dad and mum away from her but expect her to call a strange man 'father', just because that man wanted to be God's ambassador on earth.

Sinead made her way to the beach and watched the other scavenger hunters. There were about five or six along the edge of the shoreline. Some walked up and down the beach, and two looked very excited with their finds.

Sinead walked along the seashore. There was a lot of wood and metal washed up onto the beach; most of it was probably from old shipwrecks sucked up from the bottom of the ocean by the tornado.

She walked further down, away from the harbour and nearer to rough jagged cliffs. In the distance, she could see a dark-haired boy; he seemed excited as he jumped up and down, waving his hands in the air.

She noticed something by his feet but could not work out what it was. Sinead looked around to see if anyone else was paying attention to the excitement that was happening on the far side of the beach. But no one was. People were engrossed in what they had found.

Sinead looked back in the direction of the dark-haired boy, who was still waving and shouting, but apparently, she was the only one in hearing range. With a deep sigh, she walked in his direction.

"This better be good," she muttered, strolling across the beach, away from the harbour and towards the cave.

The boy had now stopped jumping, but she could see there was something on the ground by his feet; it was hard to make it out. Sinead paused, this could easily be some kind of trick. She looked around for the other scavenger hunters, but they had moved further up the beach, towards the harbour. With the ocean on one side, and the jagged cliff edge on the other, Sinead realised she was on her own. A rush of isolation and vulnerability ran over her. The boy walked towards her. His shoulder length dark, curly hair blowing in the wind. He was dressed in green Khaki, and a red T-shirt with an image on it that she couldn't work out. Neither could she understand what he was saying, but it didn't stop him; he was quite animated as he spoke, with his hands pointing to the ocean, and back to whatever lay on the ground. Sinead started to feel afraid; this guy was not dressed for the Irish weather and looked totally out of place. She quickly scanned the surrounding ground; some driftwood washed up on the beach near her foot. Sinead grabbed the wet plank of timber and held it up in front of her.

"Don't think I won't use this if I need to," she shouted, wielding the wood like it was a sword. "Just so you know, I've fought guys bigger than you."

"No, no, please help!" he held his hands in the air, as if he was ready to surrender.

"So, what do you want?" Sinead demanded.

"The seal, it's a baby, it's hurt, and needs help," the boy said now looking nervous as Sinead held a wet plank of driftwood three inches from his face.

Sinead looked at the boy, looked at the bundle on the ground, and looked back to the boy, before walking cautiously over to the bundle on the ground. It was a dark blue quilted jacket that lay on the sand. A little black shiny nose poked out through the neck. Bending down, Sinead took a closer look. It was a seal - a baby seal.

"It has a big cut by its fin; we need to get it to a vet," the boy explained, as he tried to pick up the injured seal pup.

"We don't have a vet here on the island, but I'm sure the doctor will take a look at him," Sinead said as she put her arms under the seal's lower half. "It's a bit of a walk but we should be able to manage it together".

"Thank you," the boy said. "My name is Kiel."

"I'm Sinead."

"Sin... ad," he repeated slowly.

"Sin... *aid*," Sinead repeated with more emphasis on the *aid*.

"It's a lovely name," Kiel said

"Thank you," Sinead smiled as she noticed his hazel eyes twinkling in the sunlight.

"You don't look like a Kiel."

"Oh really? what do I look like?"

"More like a Cory, a surfing kind of guy."

"Because everyone that surfs is called Cory," Kiel said, in a matter-of-fact tone, but the look in his eye showed he was teasing.

"Do you want me to show you where the doctor's office is?" Sinead pretended to be annoyed.

Kiel smiled his flawless white smile.

"Let's get this poor little one to the doctor," Sinead said, and they both picked up their pace and walked up the beach towards the harbour, and up Beach Road towards the doctor's office.

After dinner, Sinead went to her bedroom. She pulled her bed away from the wall, tapped lightly on the wood just underneath the window ledge, and a gap appeared in the wooden panels. Sinead slowly prized the panel open, reached inside with her right hand, and pulled out a black carrier bag. She sat on her bed and took out the contents of the bag: a red cotton cloth, neatly wrapped around a hand-painted wooden box. She ran her finger over the painting, running it up the green stem, and round the petals of the red rose. Sinead carefully opened her precious treasure box; this treasure would never be washed up by the ocean. Inside was a photo of her with her parents, sitting on the beach in front of the sandcastle she had built with her dad. Six-year-old Sinead sat between her parents, hugging them both, and smiling, as they posed for the camera on their annual family holiday. The last family holidays.

Underneath the photo sat a pink covered book. Sinead opened the book and gently ran her fingers through the pages, stopping at a blank page, where she started a new entry.

April 12th; Sinead started to write, in the quietness of her room; she sat on her bed and told her parents about her day.

Dear Mam and Dad,
Gran and I are well.

We had some frightening weather last night, a tornado swept across the Atlantic Ocean and it missed the island by ten miles. At one point, I thought the wind would rip the window from my bedroom wall. It howled and crashed so much, I found it scary. It hit part of the mainland and a lot of boats on the south-west coast got damaged. This morning the sun was shining, and the sky was clear, like nothing happened.

After breakfast I went down to the beach; there I met a boy named Kiel; he doesn't live here, I think he is visiting from Europe. We rescued a baby seal and took it to Dr Connor's surgery. The poor little baby had a big cut near its fin and had to have about twenty stitches. Dr Connor said it was very lucky we found him when we did, or it might have lost a lot of blood and died. Kiel is the real hero; he was the one that found it and asked me if I could help. So, the baby seal will have to stay with Dr Connor while it gets well. I don't know what will happen after; maybe I could adopt it.

Oh, and other exciting news: we are going on a trip to New York. This will be my first trip outside of Ireland with Gran. I know I went once with you both when I was little, I don't remember it. Sorry, I wish I did. But I'm glad I'm going with Gran; she deserves a real holiday.

Tomorrow, I'm going to talk on Skype with my cousins; Kailum, who lives in England, and Yolanda, she lives in Germany, and then there's Elicia from New York. It's her First Communion. I've never met Elicia, we talk on Facebook and Skype, that's how we all keep in touch nowadays. We use the computers to type messages or talk to each other via video. You would love it Dad, nobody writes long letters anymore and send them by snail mail; we use email and it's super quick.

I wish you were here, and we could do this trip together; the four of us, and we could go and explore New York and see the Statue of Liberty and skate in Central Park.

I hope you are having a nice time in heaven and the days are not too long, and you get to talk to God. Gran misses you very much, and I miss you every single day, I wish God would have let you stay here on earth with us.
Your Loving daughter

Sinead

Sinead placed the family photo in between the pages of her pink diary. She closed the book, put it back in the box, which was carefully covered in the plastic bag, returned it to its hiding place, and pushed her bed back into its original position.

She picked up a large sketchbook from her desk and headed downstairs to the front room where her gran was sitting by the fireplace, knitting fingerless gloves. Sinead sat opposite Gran on the big armchair and opened her sketchbook.

"I've had some ideas that we could add to the summer collection," Sinead said, sounding business-like, as she turned the pages of her book which also had a selection of fabric and wool samples glued to the page.

Gran looked over the rim of her glasses, looking at her granddaughter's collection of floral, checks, and tweed fabrics, that were carefully pasted into the big brown notebook. She carried on knitting, gradually crafting the yellow wool, single cable knit glove.

"They look very interesting, dear, and what designs have you created for us?" Gran asked as she continued knitting.

"Well, I was thinking we could add some accessories to our summer collection." Sinead pointed to several buttons and ribbons on a drawing of a headband in her sketchbook.

"This will add a little individuality to some headbands we made for the summer, even a little tweed fabric would give a Western Ireland signature look to it."

The fire crackled as orange and red flames danced around the black coal, which sat obediently in the centre of the fireplace, spreading its heat like long tentacles stretching across the living room, enveloping grandmother and granddaughter in its warmth and love as they sat working through the night on the various accessories of gloves, scarfs, and headbands that they made for the island gift shop.

Next morning it was time for church. A small crowd casually walked up the road, sharing their normal Sunday pleasantries, remarking on the drastic changes to the weather. Not much happened on the island that didn't go unnoticed, it was part of life in a small community.

Everybody entered the church, sat quietly in their seats, and then stood up automatically when two altar boys entered the nave, followed closely by Father Padraig and Father Brian as they walked across the front of the congregation to take their individual seats at the side altar, joining in with the choir as they sang the opening hymn.

Father Padraig started the service; it was pretty much the same every Sunday: the same prayers the same style format. Sinead could stand, sit and kneel on cue - without ever listening to a word being spoken. She stared down at the little newsletter, but the information did not sink in; they were words on a page, words she paid little or no interest in. Father Padraig prayed for someone who had died in New York, but Sinead didn't know who this person was; they had moved from the island before she was born, but now they would return and be buried in the little cemetery overlooking the sea. New York; at the mention of the name, Sinead's thoughts drifted to the tall buildings, the fashionable stores, the famous streets and parks. She would be there soon, and tonight she would talk with her cousins on Skype, and make plans about the things they could do, and the places they could see.

Father Padraig's voice started to gradually rise and fill the building. He was in one of his very passionate sermons: "if you die, where will you go?" Did one really think they would go to heaven? We shouldn't assume so, especially if we didn't pray and make the effort to be a good child of God. He gave us so much, but we take him for granted. Some of us could very happily go from one Sunday service to the next without ever giving God a thought. Then there is unforgiveness: anyone that can't forgive will never get to heaven.

"He pulls no punches," a voice from behind Sinead whispered. "Father Padraig gets straight to the point."

Sinead could feel the anger rise within her; she always felt angry when she thought of her parents. God had taken her parents from her when she was little, and it was just so unfair. Her gran sat next to her praying quietly. Gran loved God. She spoke to him every day, even if she was doing her gardening, she would talk to God as she worked. She thanked Him for Sinead and asked Him to watch over her granddaughter. She asked him to watch over her daughter- and son-in-law who were in heaven with Him.

Sinead knew if anyone in the church or on the Island would make it to heaven, it would be her gran. She loved her gran and wished she knew for certain she could make it to heaven herself, but she probably wouldn't; she spent far too much of her time being angry with God. How could she ever get to heaven if she was angry at God himself? It was a well-known fact on the Island that she used to be a disturbed, angry little girl, but when Sinead realized what people said and thought about her behaviour upset her gran, she made the extra effort of hiding her feelings. She became a loner and spent most of her time at home helping her gran make knitted accessories to sell in the gift shop, or she would hang out on the beach, dreaming about the day she would leave the Island forever. Even when she died, she would never *return* to be buried; not like that person from New York.

After church was finished, Sinead gave her gran a kiss; she was going for a walk down by the beach and would be home in time to help make dinner. Sinead found her usual spot by the sand dunes. There she lay down and stared up at the sky; this was her hiding place when she was upset or wanted to be alone. She stared up at the sky for a while and watched the clouds float by; occasionally one would float in front of the sun, causing a cool chill in the mid-afternoon air. Sinead lay there quietly; in the distance she could hear excited voices of people heading towards the harbour.

On the outside Sinead looked calm and quiet; inside there was an explosion of thoughts and anger. Anger directed at God.

"You couldn't let me be happy for a few hours, just leave me with happy thoughts! No, you had to make sure Father Padraig reminded me of how I won't get to heaven because I don't pray. No, I'm going to call him Padraig. Why am I expected to call him father, when you've taken my dad and mam from me, and left me here by myself? I know this is a tiny island and you probably don't even see it from your big beautiful kingdom in heaven, but I'm still here, and I will always be here to remind you that you left me an orphan. I had two lovely parents, and you took them away from me. At some point, you will take my gran and leave me all alone."

She took a deep breath; she could never seem to control her anger, no matter how hard she tried. She also knew she couldn't vent in front of adults because they already called her slightly disturbed and this upset her gran.

Sinead went to the beach and there, hidden among the sand dunes, she could shout at God because the crashing of the waves would drown out the sounds of her voice, and no one would hear her. God himself probably couldn't hear her, but at least she got to say what she wanted to say. After, she felt a little lighter inside, and she could go back to acting normal again.

After Sunday dinner gran went to have her little nap, and Sinead sat at the computer, ready to Skype her cousins.

CHAPTER 2
Kailum Lee

"Kailum, your dinner is ready," a female voice travelled from the kitchen, up the stairs and across the landing. It stopped outside the bedroom door where an obvious sign said "Do not enter". The voice lingered outside the bedroom door.

"Are you serious? Take that! It's mine, all mine!" shouted the voice of an 11-year-old boy as he jumped up and down on the bed.

"Kailum," a female voice called again. The voice was ignored as Kailum carried on doing his victory dance on his bed. The bedroom door opened followed by the sound of a stern male voice.

"Kailum, your mother is calling, why are you not downstairs at the dinner table?"

"I'm sorry dad," Kailum pulled off his headphones, "I didn't hear mum."

"Of course not, you are always busy playing computer games," Mr Lee said, following with other words in Cantonese. Kailum's reaction was automatic; he jumped off his bed, put his game on pause, placed his headphones by the side of his TV, and sat at the kitchen table before his dad reached the kitchen door.

"He's always playing on his XBox, it's not good," his dad complained as he sat at the kitchen table.

"I know, dear," Kailum's mum agreed sympathetically with her husband, "but I'd rather have him safe in his bedroom, and not outside in the streets. London is not that safe anymore."

"He should have another hobby, maybe football."

"I don't like sports," Kailum objected.

"During the holidays, you will need to go to summer camp. It doesn't have to be sports," his mum said.

"But I'm nice and safe in my bedroom, you said."

"Don't argue dear; your father is right, you need something else other than computer games," Kailum's mum said, passing a bowl of rice to her 11-year-old son. "You have between now and the holidays to decide what you want to do."

Kailum pulled a defeated look as he played with his food.

"Growing up in Hong Kong, I didn't go camping or play games in my bedroom, I went to work every day with my father, after school and in the holidays," his dad told him. This was not new information; Kailum had heard this story many times before, more than he cared to remember. More times than he had played any of his games.

Mrs Lee saw the defeated look on her son's face; life was very different today compared to when both she and her husband were children.

"I've got very exciting news," his mum said smiling.

Kailum looked up at his mum, but his facial expression didn't change. He looked back to his plate and carried on eating his food. He could get back to his game as soon as he had finished eating and had helped his mum clear away the dinner dishes.

"I've been talking with your Aunty in New York," his mum continued, ignoring her son's silence. "Remember your cousin Elicia? Well, she is having her first communion soon, and everyone's invited."

"Everyone?" Kailum had a vague look on his face.

"Your gran and your cousin from Ireland, your aunty, uncle, and cousin from Germany, and us. You know what that means, don't you?" his mum sounded excited.

A chance to buy lots of new games, Kailum thought to himself, maybe even ones not available in the UK. He thought it better not to share that information with his parents but gave his mum his curious innocent look. It always worked.

"A family reunion!" she said in a high pitch excited voice.

"How long are we going for?" Kailum couldn't hide his excitement as he sat up in his chair and leaned towards his mum.

"Two weeks, maybe a little longer if possible," his mum's voice was still high pitched. "Daddy can only come for a week," she added, her voice dropped to a disappointed tone.

"Closing a business for two weeks is not good," his dad explained, "But we will have lots of fun the week I am there," he smiled at his son.

"We can go to the Statue of Liberty, the Empire State Building, and Grand Central Station" Kailum said.

"And a baseball game," his dad said as he took another bite of food.

"Baseball?" Kailum looked at his dad.

"Trust me, son, it's a fun game to watch live, great atmosphere," his dad smiled.

"You can Skype your cousins this evening, and you guys can talk about the trip," his mum suggested.

Just then, Kailum remembered his cousins were girls. He was the only boy surrounded by girls.

All girls would want to do is shopping and talk about boy bands. He looked at his dad and realised a baseball game with his dad was the best plan so far. Then again, shopping meant he could go to game shops, the heaven of all devoted computer gamers. It also meant having a lot of spending money. His own personal spending money.

"Dad, you know how you always tell us how you worked for your dad as a child?"

"Yes, I worked very hard," his dad added while he cut a piece of chicken.

"Well, I was thinking," Kailum chose his words. "You will have a lot of extra work on your hands, you know, getting ready for this trip. So, you will need extra help."

"Yes, you're right," his dad paused with a piece of chicken resting on his fork, centimetres away from his mouth, as he thought about his son's suggestion. Kailum's mum looked up from her plate of food but said nothing. She hadn't thought about the extra work this trip would add to their very busy schedule.

"I could help, I could do a lot of little jobs, so you and mum could concentrate on the big jobs."

Mr Lee thought for a moment; they may have a little takeaway and not a big fancy restaurant, but it was the busiest takeaway for miles around. He didn't even like closing it down for a week, but it was important to have family holidays.

"Mm, so how much do you charge an hour?" his dad asked in a business-like manner.

"I'll get back to you on that," Kailum putting on his business voice.

He needed to look up the games online, and check the prices, and decide how many he would want to get. He might use his dad's own advice to help him earn extra pocket money, but he wouldn't be greedy, after all, they were his parents, and they were paying for the trip.

Kailum finished his food and remained seated his mum excused him from the dinner table. He rested his knife, fork and water glass on his plate, then picked them up and carried them to the kitchen sink. He scraped any leftovers into the bin, before loading the dishwasher. His mum followed him to the sink and cleared the remaining leftovers from both her husband's and her own plate into the bin before carrying on with tidying the kitchen after dinner.

She nodded a smile to her son, knowing he was waiting to carry the rubbish bag to the large dustbin outside. Within seconds the bin was empty, and the kitchen door that led down the steps to the shed was pulled shut. Kailum wanted to get his evening chores done; he had a lot of planning and thinking to do. He unlocked the shed door and put the rubbish bag into the big silver bin. From over the side of the garden wall he could hear whistling.

Leaving the stench of the shed behind he walked from the side of the house to the garden wall; he could still hear the whistling but couldn't see anyone.

"Billy?" he called out, but there was no answer; even the whistling had stopped. "Billy?" he called one more time, but there was no response.

"Whatever," Kailum said into the air, as he turned around and walked up the steps to his own back door. Just then, something flew past his head, a screwed-up piece of paper landed on the step next to him. Kailum bent down and picked it up. Spreading out the crumpled page, the note said: "I'm grounded, text me."

Kailum looked up at the second-floor bedroom window of the house next door. He pulled a funny face, and then did a fake belly laugh, picking his moment to tease Billy. It was then he realised he had not locked the shed door. Billy, the loser, had distracted him, Kailum thought to himself as he ran back to the shed and locked it. One thing he didn't need, was a city fox getting in and rummaging through the bin, causing a mess, that would get him grounded and lose any little privileges he had. With the shed locked, he headed back into the house and upstairs to his room and texted his friend straight away.

"So, what did you do now?" was Kailum's first question; he sat for a few moments on his bed waiting for a response.

"Got internal exclusion," a response came back. Grey text on his phone said Billy was typing, so Kailum waited.

"For setting off the fire alarm at school."

"That was you?" Kailum couldn't type fast enough, he had assumed that Wednesday's fire alarm was just a drill, although they didn't have two in the same week.

"No, it wasn't me; I just got the blame for it," Billy texted back.

"They can't blame you for something you didn't do," Kailum felt bad for his friend.

"Well, there's no justice in the system for some of us," Billy said, followed with an angry emoji symbol.

Billy got into trouble at school regularly, even for things he didn't do; he had a reputation, but Kailum knew he was a decent kid.

Kailum had only been in year seven for a couple weeks when some older boys picked on him and made life in secondary school miserable, but it was Billy who had jumped in and defended him. They weren't any of the kids he went to junior school with, but the boy next door, Billy, the one branded a troublemaker, made it very clear that if anyone messed with Kail, they messed with him. "We have to stick together, right Kail?" Billy said as they walked home together that day.

No one had ever shortened his name before and Kailum wasn't sure why Billy had done it, but Kailum, or Kail as he became known as at school, didn't care. Billy stuck up for him and made his life at school easy and had turned out to be a cool friend.

CHAPTER 3
Yolanda Kreitler

"Mama, I need to ask you something!" Yolanda shouted as she walked towards the big red gate. A nudge from behind made her trip, lose her balance and stumble.

"Stop it," she sounded irritated. "It's as much for you as for me," she said in a low voice. The nudge turned to a nuzzle near her armpit. Yolanda turned around, "I love you too; you are my best friend, Marco," and she threw her arms around his neck and hugged him. After a few moments, Yolanda freed her arms and reached for the large red latch and slid it back from the holder in the wooden fence, releasing the gate. It made a tired old creaking sound as it gradually swung open onto a wood chip driveway.

"Mama," Yolanda called again. Parents always had selective hearing, especially when they were being asked something. Her mum waved hello as Yolanda and Marco walked through the open gate. Her mum grabbed the edge of the gate and pushed it shut.

"Did you have a good hack?" her mum asked pushing the latch back into place.

"Yes, it was lovely," Yolanda said, "but we do need a new saddle, Mama," Yolanda patted Marco as she put the emphasis on *we*.

"What's wrong with this one?" her mum asked, playfully tickling Marco's ear.

"The strap is wearing here, and cutting into his tummy," Yolanda showed the aggravated skin near the worn strap.

"Oh, you poor little love," Yolanda's mum said as she ran her hand over Marco's tummy, stroking his irritated skin. Marco tossed his head and neighed in agreement.

"Well, I will talk to Daddy tonight," her mum said.

"Mama, it's important that we get one soon; Marco and I have so much work to do," Yolanda put on her professional voice.

"It is very hard to get him to jump if the strap is hurting him. We need a new saddle for the competition in the summer."

"Yes, I know dear, and as I said, I will talk to Daddy tonight," her mum repeated.

"I've got good news," her mother continued. Yolanda walked on the right side of her horse looking towards her mum over Marco's slender, toned back.

"I've been talking to your aunt in New York," her mum smiled, "we are all going on a vacation together."

"Who are we? When do we go? And how long?" Yolanda asked showing no emotion.

"Well your cousins in Ireland and England, your gran and aunties, and your uncles of course," her mum paused to see her daughter's reaction. Only a raised eyebrow was all Yolanda was offering as they walked towards the stable.

"It is May, so don't worry; it won't affect any of your competition dates," her mum reassured her.

"For how long?" Yolanda asked.

"Two weeks, possibly."

"Two weeks!!" Yolanda raised her voice in shock, startling Marco, who jerked his head back and tried to free himself from Yolanda's grip.

"Wooh boy, wooh, it's ok," she patted him reassuringly. "Mama I can't be away for two weeks. That's too long to be away from Marco, and it's a crucial time in our training."

"Yolanda, it's crucial to spend time with your family and interact with people. You spend far too much time being solely with animals. It's just not healthy," her mum said in a firm voice.

"Marco is not just an animal. He is very important and valuable to me. We are a team. He knows me better than anyone else on the planet." Yolanda turned and stomped off towards the stables; Marco nuzzled her ear, tipping her hat to one side.

"You even understand when I'm upset, don't you?" she patted him on the neck.

"My exact point," her mum mumbled to herself as she walked towards the house, knowing her 12-year-old daughter would spend the rest of the afternoon in the stables, partly sulking and partly fussing over Marco while clearing out his stall.

Yolanda marched into the stables, with Marco obediently walking behind her. She tied his reins to a hook just by his stable door. She started to remove his saddle and rested it on the bench. She mumbled to herself as she took off his blanket and placed it next to his saddle.

"Two weeks in New York. What can I possibly do for two weeks in a brick jungle?" Yolanda said as she picked up a stiff dandy brush from a shelf that was stocked with Marco's grooming kit. "Two weeks indeed," she said as she gently started to groom the horse. "You don't want me to go away for two weeks, do you boy?" she asked Marco, as she patted his neck. Marco turned his head towards her and nudged her arm as if in agreement.

"You are the only one that understands, you are more intelligent than most humans I know."

Yolanda gave Marco a congratulatory pat on his nose, then picked up a black plastic bucket and walked out to the yard turned on the tap and filled it with water. Yolanda stood with her arms folded as the water flowed, filling the bucket. She gradually let her eyes drift across the yard towards the house. She could see her mother through the kitchen window, busy moving from the cupboards to the kitchen table and then to the cooker, where she stood for a short while. Yolanda watched her, knowing that this was her mother's world: cooking, cleaning, and keeping the family home looking nice. Suddenly, her mum looked towards the window; Yolanda swiftly turned towards the tap, turned it off, picked up her bucket, and marched back to the stable. Placing the bucket in front of Marco, she let him drink. She walked back to the yard, filled a bowl with more water and returned to the stable. She took the stable rubber from the grooming shelf and put it in the bowl squeezing out the excess water, then gently washed Marco as he drank.

"Mama just doesn't understand business," Yolanda continued, as she washed Marco, "I'm going to have to phone Papa; he will understand." But Marco was busy drinking and didn't respond. "He will understand the importance of not having such a long break from training." Yolanda reassured herself. "I'm going to phone him now," she announced to Marco who was still busy drinking his water. Yolanda patted the distinctive white mark that stretched from his eyes to his muzzle. She walked to the grooming shelf and picked up her mobile phone, sliding her finger over the bar, and entering the code number to unlock it.

"Papa," she said, and within seconds she could hear it ring, then a woman's voice answered, "Mr Kreitler's line."

"I need to talk to my papa," Yolanda said without introducing herself.

"Hello Yolanda, Mr Kreitler is in a meeting; can I get him to call you back in twenty minutes?" a gently-spoken female said on the other end of the phone.

"Ok, danke Annaliesa" Yolanda responded, she knew it paid to be polite to her papa's secretary; plus, she liked Annaliesa; she knew horses, and had ridden in competitions when she was Yolanda's age.

Yolanda hung up her phone and busied herself clearing out Marco's stable, and put in fresh bedding. Then, she fixed up a meal for him and refilled his bucket with water. She took a hoof-picker from the grooming shelf and spoke to Marco in a reassuring voice, as she ran her hand gently from the top of his shoulder to his fetlock and picked up his foot. With the hoof picker, she dug from heel to toe removing any grit and dirt, taking care not to hurt the tender part of Marco's foot. Yolanda had just finished the third foot when her phone rang, it was Papa.

"Guten tag honig," Papa said.

"Papa, you need to explain to Mama: two weeks in New York is far too long for me to be away from Marco, and training."

"Honig, it's important for us to have quality family time too,"

"But Papa, two weeks!"

"It will be great; you will have the opportunity to spend time with your cousins and get to know them better."

"Papa, I have a very important competition coming up; I need to focus, and Marco needs a new saddle."

"I understand honig, and he will get one, I promise, and you can get new riding gear, I hear New York is great for shopping."

"Papa, thank you; it sounds lovely, but I do need to train as well."

"You know, I have an idea honig, why don't we visit a riding stable while we are in New York and we can take your cousins, I will talk to your aunty and organise it. So, I do not want to hear any complaining, we will have a lovely holiday and Marco will have rested by the time we come home. I will see you at dinner tonight. Tschuss honig,"

"Tschuss Papa."

Her dad hung up; Yolanda looked defeated as she looked at Marco.

"Well apparently, I must leave you for two whole weeks," she said with her arms around her horse's neck hugging him tightly, although it was Yolanda that needed the hug more than Marco. She pulled herself away and picked up the hoof-picker and cleaned Marco's last foot, then settled him into his stable for the night. She refilled his water bucket before heading back to the house.

CHAPTER 4
Elicia Lawrence

"Mommy, mommy!" repeated two very excited little voices, as they burst through the front door of their New York apartment.

"Hello, my babies, did you have a good time at the park with Daddy?" enquired a voice from the kitchen.

"We went to the batting cages, and I hit the ball, Mommy, four times. Four times, Mommy, that's my age, and I did it like this," said the blonde-haired, four-year-old boy, swinging his arms back and forth as he demonstrated his swinging technique.

"That is so good honey," his mommy put her arms out for a kiss and a hug. "Elicia honey, did you play as well?" mommy turned her attention to her eight-year-old daughter standing by the kitchen door.

"I played for a while, but then Lucy came, and we went and played on the swings together," said Elicia, who had blonde hair similar to her brother, which fell below her waist. Her hair was so long, people often asked her if it was real. Mom held out her arm for her daughter to join in the group hug. The scent of apple drifted up her nose as she pulled both her children against her, encircling her arms around them. Hugging them as if she had not seen them in weeks.

"Ok, wash your hands and tell Daddy dinner is ready," Mom whispered as she kissed both of them on their cheeks. The children squealed with laughter as they ran to the bathroom and called to their dad to come and wash his hands.

Mom busied herself plating the food and placing it on the dining table. From behind she got a huge hug and a kiss on the cheek.

"Dinner smells amazing," her husband said.

"Thank you," her smile was warm, but a light red rim around the corner of her eyes showed how tired she was.

"Take a seat," he said, nodding to the chair he had just pulled back from the table.

"I need to get the kids out of the bathroom," his wife replied.

"They will be fine for five more minutes," her husband's voice sounded concerned. "You look extremely tired; did you contact everyone in your family?"

"Yeah, it took a while, but I got hold of everyone, and they are all coming. I need to organise the accommodation and book a venue for the party," she said, filling the kid's glasses with milk. "I need to go into the city tomorrow and get Elicia's dress; the shop phoned, and the alterations have been done."

"Sure, I'll take Ethan to a ball game in the afternoon, he will love that," her husband said. "Who thought so much planning would go into a child's First Communion day?" he sighed.

"Can you just imagine the wedding day?" his wife joked, and they both laughed.

"What are you laughing at?" Ethan asked, running to the table.

"Nothing. Have you washed your hands?" his dad asked.

"Yes."

"Me too," Elicia said, following her brother and sitting on the chair next to her mum. "I don't know why grown-ups always laugh at nothing," Elicia sighed, "I bet it's not even funny."

"Well young lady, tomorrow afternoon, you need to talk to your cousins on SKYPE, and you cannot leave it too late, or the others will be in bed asleep."

"They're going to be in bed early!" Ethan exclaimed in surprise and then laughed.

"It's because of the time difference," his dad explained, "remember, we showed you on the map where Europe is, and that's where they live. It's nighttime there when it's afternoon here."

After dinner, mummy put the dishes in the dishwasher. "Elicia," she called from the kitchen. From the bedroom, she could hear the excited voices of her children as they played with their toys. "Elicia, it's time to get ready; you have religious study class in one hour." The sound of laughter from the bedroom made her doubt if her daughter was even listening. She took a deep breath before calling her daughter one last time. Suddenly the bedroom door opened, and the sound of little feet could be heard running down the hallway. Ethan popped his head around the kitchen door.

"Where are you going, Mommy?" he asked eagerly.

"To Elicia's school, honey," mommy answered, as she closed the door to the dishwasher and switched on the machine.

"I'm staying with Daddy," he announced, confident of his decision. "Elicia, Mommy said you have to go to school!" he shouted, as he ran back to his bedroom.

"I know, Ethan, that's why I'm getting changed!" Elicia said impatiently to her little brother, as she pulled out another outfit from her wardrobe. She wanted something pink to wear; she pulled out a skirt covered with different coloured flowers; yellow, blue, white, and pink ones. It would go perfectly with her pink Hello Kitty T-shirt, the one with Kitty holding a yellow flower. Elicia decided she needed her yellow ankle socks with the lace trim to complete her outfit. She hunted through her sock drawer, but her yellow ankle socks were not there.

Elicia pulled on her T-shirt and skirt, and with her hairbrush in hand, and a yellow scrunchy wrapped around her wrist, she called to her mum as she ran to the kitchen.

"I can't find my yellow ankle socks, Mommy; the ones with the lace on them."

"And do they have to be yellow?" Mommy asked, as her eight-year-old approached the kitchen.

Elicia stood in the doorway with a disappointed look on her face. "Well, I guess they could be white or blue."

Her mommy pulled out a fresh pair of clean socks from the pile of neatly folded laundry.

"Or could they be yellow?" her mom smiled holding up a pair of yellow socks, "pop on your socks and shoes and then I'll do your hair." Saturday school was uniform-free, and Elicia's mommy knew that the girls decided which colour to wear each week; this was the time when they were free to express their individuality.

Fifteen minutes later both Elicia and her mom were in the car driving towards Elicia's School.

"Mommy, is grandma coming from Ireland for my first communion?" Elicia asked, as she sat in the back seat looking out the window.

"Yes, honey, and your cousin Sinead," her mom said, keeping her eyes on the road. She remembered that Sinead, although older than Elicia, loved fashion too, and appeared to have a flair for designing outfits. Both girls would get on well.

"I think I might have to learn Gaelic," Elicia announced, "so when they come over, I can ask them what places they might like to see."

"Well, they both speak Irish and English, and they call it Irish and not Gaelic," her mom informed her.

"I know Sinead speaks English, but I wasn't sure if grandma did because I never understand what she's saying when she talks on Skype," Elicia explained. Her mom smiled to herself, as she looked in the rear-view mirror, at the concerned face of her eight-year-old. It was her gran's accent that Elicia didn't understand; although gran did mix Irish words into her sentence when she spoke, it still made sense in English.

"Dia agat," her mommy suddenly said.

"Pardon?" Elicia looked confused as she suddenly took her gaze from the street to catch her mom's eye in the rear-view mirror.

"It's how Irish people say hello," her mom said, saying it again, more slowly for her daughter to repeat.

"Dia agat," Elicia said pronouncing the word carefully. "That's a very long hello," she pointed out.

"It means God be with you," her mom explained, Irish people always greeted others with a blessing.

"Dia agat," Elicia repeated, whispering it to herself.

"How about we learn a new word each day? I'm sure grandma would be so happy if you greet her in Irish," mom said, as she pulled into the side street just by the side entrance to Elicia's school. The other children were gradually spilling into the playground, as they waved goodbye to their parents and excitedly greeted each other.

"Dia agat," Elicia's mom could hear her daughter say as the little girl greeted her best friend Lucy, which was followed by loud laughter, as both eight-year olds walked up the steps to their school and disappeared out of sight.

CHAPTER 5
A Trip Down the Internet

The children spoke online; Sinead and Yolanda eager at the prospects of going to Manhattan and visiting the famous stores.

"Girls; that's all they ever think about, shopping for clothes and mindless girly things", Kailum thought to himself, as he rolled his eyes.

"I want to buy new games I can't get in the UK," he said. Elicia was about to answer him, when Yolanda cut in with her strong overpowering German accent.

"I want to buy a new riding hat and boots. I have a very important competition coming up in the summer. Does your mother know where to buy them?" she asked Elicia in a very firm but bossy tone.

"I'm not sure," Elicia sounded overwhelmed by Yolanda's demands.

"Can you ask her to find the best place before we arrive?" Yolanda was abrupt.

As always, Yolanda managed to make the online chat evolve around her.

Elicia giggled and Sinead put her hand over her mouth, trying to not burst into laughter.

Kailum, with a mischievous grin, doodled on the screen with a drawing app. A long-pointed triangle rapidly appeared on the screen, followed by a rough, rugged semi-circle shape, and three long black strands of hair poking out of the side, as the semi-circle sat on top of the long-pointed triangle. Elicia held her hand over her mouth trying to muffle her laughter, but tears escaped her blue eyes and fell down her cheeks. A cone shape then appeared on the screen, with another semi-circle appearing around the rim of the cone gradually coloured in black, by a large paint brush app.

Yolanda, absorbed in her requests, had not noticed the large nose and oversize pointy hat that Kailum had drawn over her video image.

"What? What is so funny?" she said, as Sinead and Elicia burst into laughter.

"Ok, I think my mum's calling me," Kailum lied, as he tried to make a quick escape before his cousin hurled abuse at him. He leaned forward to tap the off icon on his screen with his index finger. An electric shock shot up through his bones. His straight ginger hair stood on end, as his body shook, and his finger remained frozen on the screen. Luminous multiple colours swirled from right to left on the computer screen, forming a tunnel. A mini tornado sucked him in, dragging him from his seat across his desk, knocking its contents to the floor. Kailum grabbed the edge of his screen, hoping he could prevent the tornado from pulling him into cyber world. He tried to call out to his mum, but the noise of the tornado drowned out his voice. His knuckles were white as he gripped hard on the sides of the computer, his fingers slipping across the shiny surface, leaving drag marks on the screen. He was free-falling into this multicoloured cyber world, with nothing to grasp. He felt like he was looking at his bedroom through a window that had shrunk in size. His bedroom drifted further away until only a dot remained. His mum and dad rushed through his thoughts as he carried on free-falling: would he ever see them again, and would they ever be able to find him? They were not computer savvy, and any hope of his rescue faded away, just like his bedroom.

Without warning, Kailum crashed hard to the ground. A little shaken, he guessed he had had an electric shock. His computer had probably got wet. Getting to his feet and gaining his composure, he was hurled to the ground again. His cousin Yolanda landed on top of him, followed by Sinead and then Elicia. Stunned, they sat on the floor looking at one another. What had happened? How had they ended up in the same room? And more importantly, where were they?

Before anyone could get to their feet and ask a question, a huge wooden door was flung open. Two strange and oddly dressed men stood in the doorway.

CHAPTER 6

A Stranger's House

"What's going on, where did you come from?" the older of the two asked, he looked shocked. He wore odd long robes, it looked similar to a brown sack, tied with a string around his waist. A shawl with long tassels around the edge fell over his shoulders.

"Children!!" the other man exclaimed in shock. "Children," he repeated. "Where did you children come from?" he asked in disbelief.

"Come from? Depends where we are." Sinead said, looking around the large room, with floor to ceiling tiled walls, the large multicoloured window they had just fallen through had mysteriously closed back up and looked normal. Elicia look terrified and started to cry.

"It's ok, child; no one will harm you," the older man reassured her.

"Of course, you will not hurt us," Yolanda stood up and moved next to Sinead, who had her arm around Elicia, comforting her. "My father will make you pay if you do anything to us, Geiler alter Bock!" Yolanda hissed.

"We are not dirty old men, I can assure you, young lady; we bathed this morning".

"You are the ones intruding in our home," said the younger man, in a firm voice.

"Where are we?" Sinead asked, her voice slightly shaky. "One minute we are talking to each other on the internet, and the next, we are crashing through a window and ending up here."

"This is brother Enoch, and I am Moses. And your names are ….., children?" he asked in a gentle voice.

Sinead introduced them: "This is Yolanda, Kailum, Elicia and I'm Sinead."

"How could you tell them our names!" Yolanda said, looking angry as she mumbled something in German.

"Stop calling me names in German" hissed Sinead, annoyed with Yolanda.

"It is common courtesy to introduce yourselves," Moses said, "and not polite to call someone crazy, when obviously they are not," he corrected Yolanda.

"Come, children, come and have a seat," Enoch said, pointing to the row of low seats surrounding a low exquisitely carved wooden table.

"You have been through a terrifying ordeal." The old man's eyes had a soft, gentle look, as he showed the children to the seats. "Can I offer you something to eat or drink?" he asked them.

"No," Yolanda blurted.

"Yes," said Kailum. Yolanda gave him a sharp look.

"What? I'm hungry," he confessed.

"Me too," Elicia said.

Yolanda sat with her arms folded, annoyed with the others for giving in so easily to the two strangers.

"Thank you for your hospitality, but we need to get back home. So, if you could tell us where we are," Sinead said, in her best polite manner.

"You are in Jerusalem," Enoch said, surprised.

"How did we get here?" Kailum asked, flabbergasted.

"I don't know, my child. I will have to investigate," Enoch said scratching his head.

Just at that point, Moses walked back into the room with a tray of drinks and small dishes of food; he placed them on the table, and took a seat next to Enoch, opposite the children.

"I brought you a little of everything, I was not sure of your tastes in food," he said.

"I want to go home to my mommy" Elicia said, with tears in her eyes.

"Ok, where does your mommy live?" Moses asked, passing her a bowl of food and bread. "Have a taste; it's hummus," he smiled.

"Thank you. My mommy and daddy live in the Bronx," she said, sniffing as she took the food.

"The Bronx?" Enoch looked baffled.

"Yeah, in New York City," Elicia said, as she dipped her bread in the hummus.

"This Bronx you speak of, it is not in Israel," Moses said, not quite asking a question.

"Israel; is this where we are now?" Sinead asked, picking up a glass of water.

"You have asked us lots of questions, but who are you?" Yolanda said, breaking her silence, but held a stony look on her face.

"Like I said," Moses repeated, "He is Enoch, and I am Moses".

"Moses? And we are in Israel?" Sinead cut in, "You mean like Moses in the Bible?" she added.

"Yes, that is correct," Moses smiled.

"What? really?" Kailum gushed, with a load of food in his mouth. He was beside himself with excitement as he realised who they were talking to. "Wow, you did loads of cool things. You sent the locust and plagues, and you separated the red sea and killed the bad guys. You are famous!" he said, barely stopping to take a breath, and oblivious to the raised eyebrows or the surprised looks on the faces of his cousins.

"That is great, you have read the good book" Moses replied, looking pleased and sharing the same enthusiasm as Kailum.

"A book. What?" Kailum raising his voice in confusion. "What book? I watched the movie" he said feeling somewhat bewildered that anyone thought he had literally read a book. That thought alone was just crazy.

"Movie?" Enoch couldn't help asking and looked just as bewildered as Kailum.

"*The Prince of Egypt*. It's really famous." Kailum said, not hiding his excitement.

"I am flattered that I have a movie and that you watched it" Moses continued, a little thrown by Kailum's information.

"Enoch, are you in the Bible too?" Elicia asked, as she picked up a pickled green olive to eat. She had also watched the *Prince of Egypt*, and liked it, but couldn't remember the name Enoch ever being in any movie she had watched.

"Yes, my child, I am," Enoch smiled at the little blue-eyed girl with the long blonde hair.

"I don't think you have a movie or anything like that," Kailum said to Enoch, sounding apologetic. Elicia looked from Enoch to Kailum, and back to Enoch, as she dipped more bread into the hummus.

"But you are in the Bible, and that's the most important thing," she said, so the elderly man wasn't offended.

"First, we need to find out where you are from, and how you got here," Moses said, leading the conversation away from movies and back to the more troublesome point: about the children. He turned to Enoch, "it's perplexing; we need to look into this," he said, in a low concerned voice. Both men stood up to leave the room.

"Why don't you sit here and have some more food? We will return to you shortly," Enoch said to the children.

"Where are you going?" Yolanda was curt, not trusting either of them, so she ate little of their food.

"We will come back soon," Enoch tried to assure her.

"I agree with Yolanda," Sinead sided with her cousin. "We know nothing about you, and we don't know what you are planning," she sounded wary of both men, placing her food on the table.

"Well, we could say the same of you," Moses sounded defensive, but he could understand the children's point. He sat on the seat next to them and promised he would tell them what he knew if they told him some more about where they had come from.

CHAPTER 7
A World Without Children

They talked into the early hours of the morning. Elicia and Kailum had fallen asleep on the soft seating that rested against the wall of the large living room; Enoch gave Sinead a few blankets, so she tucked them both in.

Sinead and Yolanda sat at the low table and listened as both men spoke of the times they had lived in, way back thousands of years earlier when Enoch was a faithful follower of God, and the day God took him to heaven.

"Just like that!" Yolanda didn't believe them.

"My child, have you not read your Bible?" Enoch asked in disbelief.

With raised eyebrows, Yolanda's look was obvious; the two old men had no clue about the real world, and they were like two old monks, locked away, and the only thing they did was pray to God, or at least that was what she could figure out from the conversation.

"My gran told me stories about men who disappear off the earth. Nobody knew where they had gone," Sinead said, wishing she had paid more attention to her gran's Bible stories. Then remembered that they were so far-fetched that they never made sense, so she had brushed themoff as a legend or fairytale.

"What are you thinking of, my child?" Moses asked, seeing the faraway look on Sinead's face.

"Oh, something I remember my gran saying…" she paused, wondering if she should repeat it. Both men looked eagerly for her to continue.

"She said, that one day when things were so terrible in the world, God promised to send two men to tell people of His great love for them, and they encourage people to turn back to God. I guess they are his chosen men or something."

"Old people get things mixed up and confused," Yolanda sighed.

"Is it that hard to believe?" Enoch asked, taken aback by the children's lack of faith.

The girls looked at one another, not sure if they should believe these two old men, who were still, in fact, strangers.

"It's hard for us to believe there are four children here with us, yet here you are," said Moses.

"What? In Israel? You have no children, in Israel?" Yolanda narrowed her eyes to a squint as she eyed both men suspiciously.

"No, there are no children in Israel, and throughout the world," Moses answered. "In fact, what your gran said is correct. The world became so evil, that God had removed the children from the earth. That's why we can't understand why you are here with us."

"The Lord has a plan," Enoch said standing up. "We will let you children rest and speak more tomorrow."

Enoch and Moses got up from the long-walled seats. Moses picked up the extra blankets he had placed in the corner of the seating, earlier in the evening.

"It gets chilly at night-time, so you will need these," he said, passing both girls a blanket each. They both nodded a thank you.

"Go to sleep, it's late," Enoch said with a soft smile as he turned to walk to the large wooden door, that led into the big hallway. Moses nodded a good night to both girls and followed Enoch.

"I wonder what he means," Sinead said, pulling the blanket over her and staring up at the dark ceiling.

"What?" Yolanda said, in a tired half-yawn voice.

"The Lord has a plan?"

"I don't know. They are both weird, if you ask me," Yolanda said turning in towards the wall. "We need to find out how we can get home in the morning," she said into the wall, as she drifted off to sleep.

"I wonder what God's plan was when he let my parents die?" Sinead carried on, as she stared up at the ceiling. "I can't see anything amazing about a plan that leaves a child an orphan, do you?"

Sinead waited a moment, but there was no response from Yolanda.

"Yolanda, are you asleep?" Sinead's voice was just above a whisper, so not to wake the younger ones.

"Yolanda," she repeated.

A snort and a mumble of something in German was her response.

"Oh well, maybe you can answer me, God. What is your great plan? You leave children without parents, and now parents without children, and that apparently is a plan of some kind. A divine plan." Sinead hissed into the darkness. She laid on her back on the makeshift bed waiting for a response. But there wasn't one.

"Why do people spend their time talking to a God that never answers?" she said, now getting irritated with the silence of the darkness. "I'm never going to pray," she hissed in a hurt voice as tears stung her eyes. She thought of her gran, her lovely kind-hearted gran, who never said a wrong word to anyone, and prayed every day to God. Sinead turned over on her side. The room was dark; there wasn't even a streetlight to try to break through the darkness in this strange place they were in, called Israel. Sinead wished she was back home. She wished she was with her gran, watching her knit by the fireside, feeling the heat of the fire, and watching the glow of the flames, as they played games with the darkness. Tears rolled down her face, wetting the back of her hand as it cupped under her cheek. What if she never saw her gran again? And what if they never found their way home? The four of them stuck in this world. A world without children. She pulled the blanket up around her and cried herself to sleep.

CHAPTER 8
Angels Without Wings

Sinead ran as fast as she could, her heart pounding in her chest. It was pitch dark, and it was difficult to find her way along the beach, but whatever was chasing her was getting close. Her legs felt like lumps of jelly, ready to give way from underneath her. Suddenly, she was falling, falling into the deep darkness. It felt endless; there was nothing to grasp or catch to stop her fall. A jerk of her arm made her jump. She was lying down in some strange place, and a young girl with long blonde hair was standing over her. Sinead shut her tired eyes for a few moments, hoping that when she opened them again, she would be back in her bed, safe and warm. She counted in her head: "three…, two…" but before she could say "…one", her arm jerked again. She opened her eyes and shot up into a sitting position. The little girl was still there: the girl with the amazing long blonde hair stood right in front of her.

"I need to find the bathroom," an American voice said.

Sinead rubbed her eyes, blinked and looked at the little girl.

"Oh Elicia, sorry; I'll come with you and help you find it," Sinead said, in a sleepy voice. They both walked together to the dimly lit room. Sinead replayed the events of the day before, and no matter how hard she wished, it was not just a bad dream: It was all too real.

"Where do you think it is?" Elicia whispered, as they walked towards the big wooden door.

"I don't know, we'll just have to hunt around for it," Sinead whispered back, holding her little cousin's hand.

Walking across the room, they found a small wooden door to the right. Both girls looked at each other, then Sinead walked to the door, and pulled on the handle, hoping it wouldn't squeak and wake the others. The door opened and, both girls stood at the entrance for a few moments, waiting for their eyes to adjust to the darkness.

"Maybe there's a light switch," Elicia said, not wanting to wait too much longer.

"I guess," said Sinead, as she ran her hand up and down the inside wall, hoping to find a switch. Her hand fell over a thin cord. She pulled it, and a dim light started to glow. Across the walls hung various types of armour, swords, bows and arrows, shields, two long staffs, and various other weapons that the girls were not familiar with.

"I guess this is not the bathroom," Elicia said, ready to move on to the next room.

"Guess not," Sinead sighed, as she pulled on the cord to switch off the light.

The tiled floor was cold against their bare feet as they tiptoed their way into the great big hallway, where the mosaic-style tiles ran from the floor to the ceiling. Sitting on a long slim wooden table, just under the window, was a big brass candlestick. A candlestick that looked bigger than normal: it had nine candle holders.

Four on both sides and a large one in the centre. Across the hallway were three large multicoloured windows, like the ones in the big room where the children had slept. They were not the usual stained-glass windows that you found in churches, but the frosted-style glass, with various colours, telling a story. A bright, soft yellow light glowed at the top of the windows, shining down on what looked like angels dressed in pure white robes, each with a gold belt around their waist, and a gold crown on their heads; they appeared to be floating upwards. Angels without wings.

On either side of the wingless angels, stood six tall angels, with their wings unfurled to their full extent. Each angel held a trumpet upright, and appeared to play music. Sinead paused for a moment and examined the images on the huge windows.

"Wingless angels; how weird, but everything was odd and strange," she thought, but right now she was too busy to work out what the bizarre image meant. They walked down the great hallway, past the large staircase, in search of a bathroom. They peered around several doors; one led to a small empty room. The next led to a large kitchen, with a large stove and a long wooden table, but there were no other doors leading off the room. As they both turned to walk back towards the large staircase, to carry on their hunt for a bathroom, they found an inquiring Moses, standing before them.

"What are you young ladies looking for?" he asked, not surprised to find them snooping, but that it was Sinead rather than Yolanda.

"I need the bathroom," Elicia said in an urgent voice.

"It's just here," Moses pointed to the smaller room.

"Where?" Sinead couldn't hide her surprised tone. "There's nothing in there."

Moses opened the door to the small room and pointed to a wooden platform on the ground, which had a hole in the middle, covered with a stopper attached to a string.

"Just pull it," he said, pointing to the string, then directing her to the tap, he said, "fill the bucket with water to wash." Elicia followed Moses' direction as she investigated the unusual toilet in the middle of the small room. Sinead stood by the door looking from Elicia to Moses. Her only thought was that these guys were nut-jobs, whether they had movies made about them or not.

"I have to pee in a hole in the ground?" Elicia shrieked in shock, as she stood holding a long string with a wooden round stopper dangling from the end.

"Yes," Moses said.

"You don't have a real bathroom?" Sinead asked.

"It doesn't matter, I need to go now," Elicia said, shutting the door, leaving Moses and Sinead outside. Sinead didn't shift her gaze from Moses; she just stood waiting for an answer.

"A real bathroom?" he asked.

"Yeah, you know, shower, bath, and an actual toilet to sit on, that you can flush," she said with a slight hint of sarcasm in her voice.

"Is that what you children have in your homes?" Moses asked, surprised.

"Everyone has them; it's standard" Sinead said, with a hint of coldness in her tone. "I thought a hole in the ground was something from the middle ages."

"Well, I guess everyone has what is familiar to them" Moses said, walking to the kitchen. "I will fix breakfast. You and your little cousin can come and help me when you're ready." It sounded more like a command than a request.

Elicia opened the door to the small unusual bathroom.

"Did you wash your hands?" Sinead asked.

"Yes," Elicia smiled.

"Why are you smiling?"

"Oh, it's just a weird bathroom, I can't wait to see the others' faces when they see it."

Both girls laughed; Kailum might be ok; after all he's a boy, but Yolanda's reaction would be priceless.

"We're on breakfast duty," Sinead said nodding towards the kitchen. As they walked in, they found Moses cooking.

"Can I help?" Elicia asked.

"That would be lovely," Moses smiled at her, then he picked her up and sat her on the work counter next to him. "Here," he said passing her an egg. "Break the shell and pour the egg in the pan on top of the tomatoes."

"I like cooking," Elicia said.

"You are a superb cook, may I add," Moses smiled. Then, looking to Sinead, he said, "Would you mind getting the bread? It's ready." He nodded towards the stove.

Sinead grabbed a towel from the table and used it to take the warm bread from the wood burning stove.

"Do you help your mum to cook?" he asked Elicia.

"Sometimes, depending on what she is cooking: I make cookies and cupcakes with her," Elicia said with enthusiasm. Moses smiled as the little girl went on to tell him about what her mum had taught her, and how she made them at the weekend because she had a lot of homework to do on weekdays.

She told him how excited she was about her Holy Communion day, the long white dress she had picked out with her mum, the party, and how all of her family would come from different places in Europe and the USA to see her on her special day.

"It sounds very exciting," he said, as he finished stirring the food in the pan. "Ok I think everything is ready." He dished the eggs and fried tomatoes onto a plate, then placed the food and the bread on a tray, where six glasses sat. He helped Elicia back down from the counter, and all three of them carried the food to the big room.

CHAPTER 9
Angry With God

Moses and the two girls went back to the main room, where they found Enoch sitting with Yolanda and Kailum. Everyone sat around the little table and tucked into the eggs and tomatoes seasoned with herbs and spices.

"Mmm, this is so good," Kailum said, putting more food in his mouth.

"What did you mean when you said last night that God had a plan?" Sinead asked. She didn't want to wait any longer and now was as good a time as any to get answers.

The others looked at her in amazement.

"What do you mean, my child?" Enoch asked.

"Last night you said you couldn't understand why we were here. Then you said God had a plan." Sinead sounded angry, which took Moses and Enoch by surprise.

"God has a plan for all of us," Enoch explained. "We are all here for a reason; we may not know what it is yet, but we need to trust in God."

"Trust God!" Sinead almost exploded, "trust God: the same God that left my parents to die. You're saying he has a plan; what kind of plan can he have for someone that's dead?" her hand shook, as she put her glass back on the table.

"Oh no, here we go," Kailum said under his breath, as he reached across the table to get more bread.

"I don't trust or pray to God," Sinead carried on, ignoring the shocked faces and what her cousin mumbled.

"He let my parents die and left me an orphan!" she hissed. "So why would I be part of the plan if I don't even care about him or his plans, and why would he bring me or my cousins here?"

"My child, have a drink and let's discuss this calmly," Moses said, picking up her glass of water and passing it to her.

"Don't let her bother you too much, she is disturbed," Yolanda said, putting emphasis on 'disturbed'.

"No, I'm not" Sinead jumped up and glared at her cousin. Her whole body shook with anger and frustration; she was so tired of people labelling her as disturbed. She wasn't; she was just plain angry, and with good reason too.

"No, she is not disturbed," Enoch stood up and put his arm around Sinead. "She is grief-stricken, and that's ok. Just think how hard it is to be apart from the ones you love. Then imagine how it feels for Our Lord when so many of his children have turned away from him. The pain must be unbearable," Enoch said, as he encouraged Sinead to sit back down on the seat.

"Just like when Jesus died on the cross for us, that must have been painful," Elicia said.

"Yes, you're right," Moses smiled at her, while Yolanda and Kailum looked at Elicia in amazement as she joined in the discussion.

"We are born to be with God, and each of us has our own time here on earth. Some live a long time, some of us die young, but regardless of how long or short we are on this earth, we are created to spend eternity with God," Moses explained.

"What if we are not good enough to go to heaven for eternity?" Kailum asked, sounding worried.

"Good enough?" Moses looked at him, "none of us will ever be good enough."

Kailum looked a little pale; he never liked church and all that praying stuff, but this discussion was getting a little heavy and worrying.

"But people, like priests, go to heaven, don't they?" Kailum asked; now was a good time to get answers to questions he would be forbidden to ask at home.

"They do," Yolanda piped in, and using air quotes, "they're married to the church, and they pray all day long," she informed the group.

"Well I don't think I'm going to heaven," Sinead sniffed, wiping away her tears. "God is not happy with me, because I'm always angry with him, and I don't pray; even when I go to church with my gran, all I do is shout at him."

Moses and Enoch looked at each other with worried expressions on their faces. The other children looked at each other, flabbergasted by Sinead's open confession.

"Children, where do you get this information from?" Enoch broke the silence.

The children paused for a moment then glanced at one another.

"Church," Yolanda said.

"School, adults," Kailum added.

"You need to turn to the word of God," Enoch said.

"The Bible?" Elicia asked, making sure they were all on the same page.

"Yes," Moses nodded, "But Jesus said, 'suffer little children, and forbid them not, to come unto me...' "

"...For theirs is the kingdom of heaven," Elicia finished the sentence.

"Yes," Moses smiled at her. The other children stared at her.

"We can all go to heaven because of Jesus," Enoch said, "Jesus died and rose again, so we are all free to be with him in Heaven." He looked at the bewildered young faces.

"Jesus has unlocked the door of heaven for all of us," Enoch explained.

"What The Lord asks of us, all of us," Moses said, looking around at the little group, "He wants us to have a relationship with him. Talk to him every day, tell him about our worries, and ask him for help. Also, thank him for everything."

"Jesus loves all of us," Enoch added. "He died for us because he loves us, and we belong to him."

"So, there is hope for all of us? Yolanda said, looking from Enoch to Sinead and then to Kailum.

"We are all his children, so yes, all of us. We are all important to The Lord" Moses said.

"Why did he let my parents die?" Sinead asked, her voice giving away the pain in her heart.

"We don't know," Moses was gentle, "But it's understandable to be sad and miss your parents, and it's ok to tell God how you feel."

"I miss my parents," Elicia said, as she sat close to Sinead, resting her head on Sinead's shoulder.

"I do too," added Yolanda, "And we have only been away for one day; I don't think I could live every day without them." She looked at her cousin, and for the first time she understood the pain her cousin had endured for the past six years. The room was silent, as the four cousins sat and hugged each other, three understanding how the fourth had felt.

CHAPTER 10

Vanished in the Blink of an Eye

"Why did God bring us here?" Elicia asked, still resting her head on Sinead's shoulder.

"We don't know," Moses said, "But I'm sure when the time is right, The Lord will let us know."

"What if we have to stay here forever?" asked Kailum, concerned, as he looked down at his hands and scratched at an old scab on the back of his left one.

The others looked at him in horror.

"What? I'm just asking."

"We are just as baffled as you, as to why you are here," Moses answered.

"Remember, The Lord has already taken the children from the Earth," Enoch said

"Where did he take them?" Elicia asked, trying to imagine all the children on Earth vanishing, and all the schools left empty, well, except for teachers.

"To Heaven," Enoch said. "Along with some adults who were obedient to God."

"Because they all had a relationship with Jesus?" Elicia said, just to make sure she understood this whole concept of a relationship with Christ and getting to Heaven.

"Yes," Enoch smiled.

"So, when you say he took them," Kailum thought out his question before voicing it. "Well like how? Did they all die, or something," he avoided eye contact with his cousin so as not to let the horror on their faces stop him from asking the questions he had spinning inside his head.

"No," Moses smiled.

"NO!!!" all four cousins said at the same time.

"No," he repeated. "One day they all disappeared from the Earth, in the blink of an eye."

"Nobody can disappear," Yolanda jumped in. "That's impossible."

"Magicians do it all the time," Kailum objected.

"All things are possible with God," Enoch said, before both cousins could take the argument any further.

"Is it in the Bible?" Elicia asked.

"Yes," Moses said, "It's mentioned several times. When two people are working in the field, one will go and the other will stay. They will go in the blink of an eye. That is quick."

"Gran talked about that," Sinead said, "I think she has friends she talks to, about Jesus coming back on a cloud and taking people up to Heaven."

"What, like flying?" Kailum's voice was excited.

"I guess," Sinead said.

The four children looked at Moses and Enoch intrigued; people flying up to the clouds to meet Jesus, and they didn't have to die.

"Sounds like a science fiction movie," Yolanda said, "People going to Heaven without dying."

"Sounds like fun," Kailum joined in.

"It's the rapture," Moses said.

Sinead, in a far-off gaze, appeared lost in her thoughts.

"Sinead, my child, are you ok?" Enoch asked her. She looked at him a little lost.

"I was just wondering what happened to all the people that died, like my parents; what happened to them?" She said sounding worried.

"The dead in Christ rise first," Enoch said "That means the Lord calls them first, and then he will call those that are on the Earth to come and meet him in the clouds afterwards".

"It sounds like some kind of fairy tale," Yolanda said, trying hard not to be hoodwinked by these two old men they had just met.

"I think it's cool," Kailum had a wistful look in his eyes. "It would be like flying; I'd love it."

"It is in the Bible," Enoch tried to reassure Yolanda. "We can show you where it is, and you can read it for yourself."

"I think they made a movie about it," Elicia joined in the conversation again; she had sat quietly for so long, the others had almost forgotten she was there. Yolanda let out a deep irritated sigh.

"They make movies about everything, the Americans" she said.

"Well, movie ideas come from somewhere," Elicia stood with her hands on her hips, glaring at her cousin.

"Ok children," Moses said, looking like he was ready to break up a fight.

"Why does one get left in the field and one gets taken?" Sinead asked, a little troubled. The others looked at her. "The people working in the field, one gets taken, and the other is not?" She repeated herself.

"Well," said Moses, settling back into his seat. "The one that is taken was a believer and follower of Jesus; he had a relationship with Christ, and he prayed and talked with The Lord, and did what The Lord asked him to do. The other didn't."

"So, the people left behind, what happens to them?" Sinead asked, with a very serious expression on her face.

"God gives them a chance to change their ways and follow him. They are his children too, and he wants all of them to be in Heaven with Him, but they also have the freedom of choice to make that decision." Moses answered.

"But kids, you said kids get raptured. Raptured, that's what you call it," said Kailum, as he picked up the last piece of bread.

"Yes," Enoch smiled, seeing the relief on Kailum's face. "But you too can also pray and talk to The Lord about whatever troubles you, or whatever thoughts you have. It's good to build a relationship with Christ. Jesus loves you. You belong to him and his love is so powerful, more than anything else on this earth or underneath it."

"Now children, why don't you have a little rest? Enoch and I will pray in the upper room. But we have one very important rule," Moses said, pausing for a moment, looking at the four-solemn young faces. "Do not go outside, it is not safe," he said, a look of concern on his face.

Moses and Enoch rose and left the room and went to the little room upstairs. The four children sat around the table, looking at each other as they soaked up the information they had received. Suddenly, Yolanda jumped up and ran to the great hallway.

CHAPTER 11
Disobedience

Yolanda tiptoed across the room to the big wooden door, and peering around the doorway, she watched Enoch and Moses climb the stairs and disappear around the corner.

"What are you doing?" Sinead hissed.

"SSSSH," Yolanda put her fingers up to her lips.

"Don't you dare shush me!" Sinead raised her voice above a whisper, with annoyance in her tone.

"They told us to stay here," Elicia said.

By now, Yolanda was making her way through the large hallway towards the stairs. Kailum ran to the doorway and watched Yolanda go up the stairs; he wasn't sure if he should class her as the cool cousin or a basic troublemaker.

"If they catch you, you'll be in a lot of trouble," he added from the bottom of the stairs, with a hint of admiration in his voice.

"They must catch me first," Yolanda responded, sounding sharp, or was it her accent? Kailum wasn't sure.

"Don't encourage her," Sinead had joined him at the stairs followed by Elicia. Kailum looked at Sinead with raised eyebrows; his thoughts were obvious: *"Are you for real?"*

"She's being very disobedient," Elicia said in a stern voice, taking them both by surprise, as she stood with her arms folded.

Yolanda paused at the top of the stairs; in front of her were three wooden doors running along the left side of a long corridor. Sunlight flooded the hallway, pushing its way through the large window at the top of the stairs. The heat from the sun hit the back of Yolanda's neck, making her feel hot and sweaty. Her cheeks felt flushed, and the pounding of her heart was the only sound she could hear. A sweet, pleasant floral scent tickled her nose, but strangely there were no flowers or plants anywhere nearby. She scanned the corridor, and her eyes followed the stairs as it carried on its journey to the floor above. Yolanda took a deep breath and walked across the tiled floor and then stopped outside a big door for a few moments. With both hands she pushed down on the handle, holding her breath as she pushed the door. It opened with ease; light from the large window flooded the room. Inside was a bed pushed against the wall, with a folded blanket resting on top. A table at the opposite wall was home to a pile of books and an antique lamp, with a chair pushed underneath. Above the table was a small window with no curtains. It was a simple, basic room. Hooks on the wall served as a wardrobe. "*A room that only a monk would sleep in*" Yolanda thought.

She tried the next door, turning the handle and pushing it open. She froze. The door squeaked, announcing the intruder. The room was a mirror version of the first room, but the window was larger and opposite the door. Both rooms looked so impersonal; no pictures, no ornaments, not even a wardrobe or dresser for clothes.

Yolanda stood outside the third door for a short while, wondering what was on the other side. She debated with herself whether it was a good idea to enter. *"Just take a little sneak peek and see what these two old men get up to behind closed doors"*, she thought to herself. Being monks meant they probably prayed. Old people do boring stuff like that, and these two were so old they were ready to kick the bucket, so they needed all the praying time they can get.

A raised voice boomed from the other side of the door.

"Maybe they were arguing. Maybe they were arguing about what to do with her and her cousins", Yolanda thought to herself.

She tiptoed to the door; it wasn't as large or as heavy as the one in the main hallway downstairs, so she would easily hear what was being said. She pressed her ear against the door. Someone was talking out loud, but she wasn't sure if it was Enoch or Moses. Then she heard other voices. They seemed further away and sounded more like a mob.

Irritated-sounding voices could be heard bellowing from the other side of the door. Yolanda pulled on the door handle, hoping it wouldn't squeak. There was so much noise coming from the room, they wouldn't notice her. Pushing the door ajar, it slid open with no creaks or squeaks. She patted the door with a thank you for not giving her away. She was only taking a little look, and there was no harm in that. They didn't know these men from Adam, so her investigation was justified.

She poked her head around the door and looked into the room. It was small, long and narrow, with seating along the three tiled walls, but there was no sign of either Enoch or Moses. She pushed the door open a little further to get a better view. There was a large balcony window to the right, at the far end of the room. The metal doors went from the floor to the ceiling and looked similar to French windows. They were pushed open and Enoch and Moses were on the balcony. They were talking aloud, saying something about God, and about people being deceived. Yolanda did not understand what they were saying; she took a few steps into the room, just to hear them more clearly. From outside, she overheard someone shout in another language; it wasn't German or English. Moses responded as if he was answering a question.

Yolanda didn't understand what was being said, but her curiosity was getting the better of her. She ventured further into the room. To her right, next to a row of wall benches, was a huge Egyptian vase standing tall and proud. Yolanda tiptoed across the room and ducked down behind the oversized vase. She was close enough to have a view of the balcony, but still near enough to the door for a quick escape.

Moses spoke in a clear voice, while angry shouts seem to come from the street outside. A huge dark shadow fell over the balcony. Yolanda moved from behind her safe hiding place, to take a closer look. A loud high-pitched screeching sound cut through the shouting mob. Together, both Enoch and Moses spoke loud and clear; it appeared that they were praying.

The shadow seemed to shift; Yolanda crept a closer. For a moment she thought she saw a flapping of wings, giant wings, but it was impossible; dinosaurs had died a million years ago. Hot air spun passed her head, almost tearing off her ear; a flying object smashed through the

Egyptian vase, causing it to shatter into a million pieces. Flames exploded from the long, slim metal arrow buried in the wall. A second arrow flew past Moses' head and pierced the wooden window box just above his shoulder. Enoch leaned forward, bent over the balcony, towards the flying shadow. His back was to Yolanda, blocking her view, but for a moment she swore she saw a burst of flames come out of nowhere, followed by a loud high-pitched screech, as the flapping of wings echoed through the air, penetrating her eardrums. She covered both ears with her hands, protecting them from the ear-splitting sound.

Yolanda jumped to her feet and ran out the door, not bothering to shut it behind her. She ran down the stairs, to find the others standing where she left them, at the foot of the staircase in the great big hallway.

"We need to get out of here," she told them, her voice shaking. "We need to get out of here now."

"Why, what's happened?" Kailum asked, seeing the scared look on his cousin's face.

"And where do you suggest we go?" Sinead said, confused. Elicia watched, but said nothing; Yolanda may be bossy, but right now she looked scared.

"Any place but here, and now is not a good time to be explaining; just trust me, we aren't safe, so let's go." It sounded like an order, but her facial expression was pleading with them.

All three followed their cousin out of the house, running into the dusty streets outside.

CHAPTER 12
The Market Square

"Where should we go?" Sinead asked, catching up to Yolanda, who was no longer walking, but sprinting through the street. Sinead dragged little Elicia by the hand.

"Who are they shouting at?" Kailum asked, trying to keep up with the girls, but could hear an angry crowd from behind some large buildings.

"I don't know," Yolanda responded, keeping her pace and not looking back. She took a sharp left turn along a narrow street, leading away from the loud, angry shouts. Her heart was beating, as it vibrated in her eardrums; her body trembled, and her pace quickened. The others followed her; Sinead saw the scared look on Kailum's face, and Elicia was looking pale. She wanted to offer words of comfort, but what could she say? She didn't have any words of encouragement, how could she? They were lost in this strange place; how they got here was a mystery, so how could she tell them that everything would be ok?

The little group of children cut across another couple of streets and found themselves in a market square. People were busy passing through the market; others stood by their stalls, eager to sell their products.

Slowing their pace, the children looked at each other.

"It's a farmer's market," Elicia broke the silence. "Someone will help us, and we can phone home," she added with hope in her voice.

"Yeah, possibly," Sinead said, trying to keep positive.

They walked into the square, full of shoppers and traders. Sinead scanned her surroundings. So far, there was not a child in sight, but that meant nothing; they could be at school, or at home.

A loud voice thundered across the market square; a furious man pointed angrily at the children. A woman nearby shooed them away from her fabric stall.

The children looked at one another, baffled. They might not have understood him, but the sound of his voice and reaction of the other adults was enough for them to turn and run, run far away from here. They ran towards the side streets, but a group of men ran towards them, blocking their way and waving their fists in the air, shouting at the children.

Kailum quickly dived under a table full of fish, lobsters and crabs. He kicked a bucket of shellfish out on to the streets and watched as grown men slipped and dropped hard to the ground. Yolanda followed him, pushing over the table, clearing their escape route. Sinead and Elicia hid under another table behind rolls of fabric. Sinead beckoned to Elicia to follow her as she ducked between tables. As she did so, two large smelly, dirty feet stood at the end of the table, blocking her escape. She watched as Sinead ducked in and out among tables, disappearing out of sight.

Elicia crouched down by the table; she held her hand over her mouth, as tears started to flow, stinging her cheeks.

"Please God, help me," she said in a faint whisper.

She stayed there as feet ran past, in both directions. Then, another pair of feet in leather sandals stopped right beside her. She hid behind the fabric, which fell three-quarters of the way down the leg of the table. A hand pulled up the fabric, revealing the face belonging to the feet that owned the leather sandals. A terrifying looking man, with long dark knotted hair and a full raggedy beard, was staring back at her. He looked and smelled as if he hadn't showered in months. With a wild toothless smile, he reached in to grab her. Elicia screamed. A hand dragged her by the arm, in the opposite direction, away from the grasp of the toothless man. Clambering to her feet, she ran, grateful that one of her cousins had come to her rescue. Elicia looked up as she ran, but it wasn't Sinead or Kailum that held her by the arm, and it wasn't Yolanda either. It was a boy with loose curly black hair, falling to his shoulders. He looked a similar age to Sinead, but Elicia was confused; was he rescuing her or kidnapping her? Elicia whimpered as she tried to break free from his grip.

"No, no," he said. "The streets are too dangerous; we need to find somewhere safe." They ran along a narrow side street; the buildings whizzed past in a blur. They ran so fast, Elicia's feet hardly touched the ground. They ran through ten side streets, cutting across another ten or fifteen little streets. The boy came to a stop. Still holding Elicia by the arm, he pointed to an old run-down building.

"Let's hide out here," he said. He breathed easily, despite their sprint through the streets. He led Elicia into the building. They climbed up a broken staircase that led to the roof, a flat roof that gave them a view of most of the city.

"Are you ok?" he asked Elicia, in a gentle voice.

"I guess so," she whispered, "But I need to find my cousins."

"We will, I promise," he smiled a soft comforting smile, his hazel eyes twinkled as they caught the sunlight.

"Who are you?" Elicia asked, as she sat in the shade, out of the hot sun.

"Rabbi Enoch told me to come and find you," he said. Elicia felt safe at the mention of Enoch, but something had frightened Yolanda so much, that she had insisted on them leaving the house. That thought alone made Elicia feeling unnerved.

"I promise to find your cousins, but we need to wait for the crowds to disperse some more. It will be safer when it's dusk."

"Why did they do that; get so angry and attack us?" Elicia asked. Grown-ups are supposed to protect kids, not scare them or chase them, although not every adult is nice. These grown-ups were terrifying.

"The wild look on their faces should show you how frightened they were," the boy said. "To see children with blonde hair and blue eyes, is terrifying for them," he smiled.

"What about you? You're a kid," Elicia pointed out.

"Yes, but I make sure they don't see me," he smiled. They sat in the shade until evening, when it was safe to find the others.

CHAPTER 13
The Escape

"I can't believe, you are all such der trottel!" Yolanda's cheeks burned red with anger.

"Yolanda, we need to find Elicia", Sinead shouted at her.

"Find her, find her?" Yolanda shouted, now even more enraged. "It wasn't me that lost her".

Kailum took two steps back behind Sinead; his cousin sounded as if she was about to hit def-con one, or was it that German accent that made her sound more angry?

"I am trying to help, and you treat me like I am an idiot."

"No, we do not think you are an idiot" Sinead said, lowering her voice. "Given the situation we're in, it's your advice we followed and now see where we are."

Yolanda tensed up as she forced herself to take a deep breath; she noticed the distress on Sinead's face. "We will be fine, we will go back and search for her," she tried to reassure her two cousins.

"Ok we need to stick together and go back into the city when it's dark," Sinead said, a little calmer. "Splitting up is a bad idea. It's enough one of us is missing."

"Ok, we will try your way for now; when you discover you are wrong, we will try it my way," Yolanda said, leading the group across the dusty dirt road, back towards the city.

"We'll consider it," Sinead said, as she walked next to Kailum, and followed Yolanda's lead.

"What is a 'der trottel'?" he asked in a low voice to Sinead.

"It means 'jerk'," Yolanda shouted back over her shoulder "Which I am not, but for you it may be the case."

Sinead gave Kailum a sympathetic smile, then moving her lips she said, "No you're not."

It was getting dark as the little group did their return journey back to the strange, unfamiliar city.

Earlier in the day, when they had tried to escape the mob, Yolanda and Kailum had run along the street, cutting through small alleyways. Kailum, leading the way, had seen Sinead out the corner of his eye, it looked as if she was being surrounded by a group of three or four men.

He beckoned to Yolanda to stop. Holding up his right hand, and crouching behind a small wall, he put his fingers to his lips. Yolanda nodded in agreement, happy to stop and have a rest. Glancing over the wall, they saw Sinead, as she knocked over several barrels of liquid. The men that chased her appeared to be on ice skates, as they had each lost their footing on the slippery substance, falling to the ground with a thump. Sinead disappeared into a side building. Kailum and Yolanda looked at each other; Sinead was now trapped with no obvious escape route.

"There may be a backdoor," Yolanda whispered. Where they were standing limited their view, as they soon lost sight of Sinead. Kailum scanned the streets and buildings around them, checking the route that led to the building where their cousin was hiding. Keeping low and out of sight, they cut through the houses, making their way through the back streets.

"If we go through this street and cut around the back of those buildings," Kailum whispered, as he pointed to his left, "we will be out of their view." He nodded at the four men, now banging on a blue metal door that Sinead had locked.

"Are you good with directions?" he asked Yolanda.

"What? Why?" she looked confused.

"Because although we're going left, we need to bear right, and we need a high landmark to pinpoint our location," Kailum said.

"We are not in one of your computer war games," Yolanda said, annoyed.

Kailum looked at her and with raised eyebrows; his expression said: *and you think this is normal?* She let out a deep sigh as she grasped what he was saying and looked to where he was pointing.

"Over there," she pointed to a long pole on a roof with cables hanging over it. "That looks like the building we need."

"Let's go," Kailum nodded, and they both headed off, away from the loud banging and the shouting men, and through a small street that led to several rundown houses.

Sinead ran through the dark dim-lit corridor towards a small room. To her left, just inside the door was a staircase, but she needed to stay on the ground level and find another way out. Beads of sweat rolled down her face, and her damp hair stuck to her head and neck. She stopped for a moment to catch her breath; a stale damp musky stench cut through her nose and clawed at her throat. Outside, the banging and shouting carried on from the street. It felt as though half of Jerusalem had now congregated outside the door. She looked around the little dark, damp room that had once been someone's kitchen. There was no way out; a cement block sealed the window shut. There didn't appear to be a backdoor or an exit. Seeking the next room hoping to find an escape route, Sinead stood amongst the dirt and the debris. She clenched her fist, and drew a breath, staring at the sealed windows. Looking through the room, she saw a broken cupboard, some old chairs and a table. If the thick layer of dust on the furniture was anything to go by, it was obvious no one had lived here for a long time. She headed back to the front door. The men were still outside; she could hear them through the metal door.

The banging had stopped. Thick black smoke crawled its way underneath the door, and in-between the sides of the door frame and wall. It climbed upwards, like waves on a dark ocean, choking the air as it laid claim to the little hallway. Sinead took a deep breath, pulled her sleeve over the palm of her hand, using it to shield her mouth. She headed back towards the door; her heart pounded in her ears as she ran up the stone staircase.

She climbed four flights of stairs that lead to the flat roof. Kneeling on the ground, she breathed in the late evening air as she recovered from the suffocating smoke. Crouching low, she crawled alongside the small wall that ran around the length of the roof. The wall, Sinead guessed, could be shoulder high to someone her height. Across the rooftop, she saw a large pole with a loose cable dangling over the side of the building. This was her opportunity to escape; she could scale down the side of the building and hope the cable was long enough. Drawing a deep breath, she flung the cable over the side, scanning the area to make sure no one saw her. All the action was at the front of the house, and she was now at the back of the building.

The cable fell only three-quarters of the way, Sinead would have to make it work, this was her only chance to escape. She had managed to climb halfway, when she noticed two people running out of a derelict building across the street. She was trapped with nowhere to escape.

Sinead looked again, blinked twice, and let her eyes re-focus. It was Kailum and Yolanda; they stopped at the bottom of the wall and looked up, then Kailum returned to the building they had emerged from, followed by Yolanda. They returned with what looked like a long blanket or tarp, and both stood at opposite ends, pulling the tarp out to its full size. They beckoned to Sinead to jump the last quarter of her climb, and they would catch her; well maybe not catch her, but at least break her fall.

Sinead wasn't sure about free-falling the last lap of her climb. She looked at the distance between her and the safety net and the distance was a little more than she hoped. Holding the cable a while longer, she looked at her cousins far below and felt light-headed. They were beckoning to her with hand gestures.

Without warning, their gestures became more urgent as they jumped up and down. She wished they'd stop; they were making her dizzy, and she now imagined the cable was moving of its own free will.

"JUMP!!!" shouted Kailum.

"Look up!" Yolanda shouted, pointing to the roof. Sinead looked up towards the roof; there were two men at the top, reaching over and grabbing the cable. They pulled her back up the side of the house, towards the roof.

"Let go!" Yolanda shouted.

"Let go of the cable!" Kailum shouted, waving his hands in the air.

Sinead let go of the cable. The world spun for about three seconds, as she let herself free-fall down the side of the house, then everything went black.

CHAPTER 14
The Stowaways

Sinead gradually opened her eyes. Her head hurt, everything looked hazy and blurred; Yolanda was standing over her and tugging at her shoulder.

"Sinead, Sinead," Yolanda's voice was pleading.

"What happened?" Sinead asked, still dazed.

"We need to go; they'll find us soon," Yolanda grabbed hold of Sinead's arm and pulled her to her feet.

"Come, we need to go now," Kailum said urging both girls to follow him back into the derelict building, from which he and Yolanda had originally emerged. They both grabbed Sinead by each arm and dragged her through the rundown houses and shops. The buildings looked as if they had survived a war.

"We need to keep going, and keep out of sight," Kailum had an authoritative tone to his voice.

"Out of this city, if possible," Yolanda said in a low voice; she sounded out of breath as she dragged Sinead.

In theory it was good idea, but actually none of them knew where they were or the route that would lead away from the city.

Dusk was starting to settle. This made it easier for them to duck in an out of the shadows, through the various streets and side alleys. Kailum took the lead as he scanned each street and alleyway for the next best route, making sure there was no one around to catch them.

"This is crazy; we can't carry on like this," said Yolanda, as she struggled to hold up a weary-looking Sinead. "We need to find a way out of here, get on a metro or something?"

"We can't," said Kailum. "People will see us, and adults are our enemies here."

"Right, well, if they are our enemies," Yolanda argued, "then we need to take care of ourselves and find transport."

"Any kind," Kailum looked amused, as he relished the challenge. "We could hot-wire a car," he said with a smile.

"And you know how to drive?" Yolanda sounded irritated and tired. Sinead groaned as she hung from both their shoulders, dried blood stuck to the side of her head.

"We have to keep her moving," Yolanda said, as she took a step forward to carry on with their journey.

They walked through the streets. It appeared this side of the city had no residents, just a few rundown buildings. When they reached the corner, they heard shuffling, and something being dragged. Kailum held up his free hand and, with a clenched fist, he signaled for them to stop. He leaned Sinead against the wall, and quietly crept to the corner of the street. Then he hunched down as he turned the corner. Yolanda followed him. There, they spotted a man with an open-backed truck; he appeared to be delivering something.

"I have an idea," said Yolanda, "It may be our only chance. When he has gone inside, let's jump on the back and hide under that white tarp." Kailum looked at Yolanda and then at Sinead, contemplating his cousin's idea.

"It may be our only chance to put distance between us and this place, and she is virtually a dead weight," Yolanda whispered, as she nodded towards Sinead. Kailum nodded in agreement.

The driver pulled a big heavy looking barrel off the back of his truck; it would probably take him a while to carry it inside, giving the children time to hide in the back of his truck.

As soon as the driver was out of sight, they both grabbed hold of Sinead and got ready to run to the truck.

"You will have to run!" Yolanda whispered in Sinead's ear.

Sinead nodded in agreement.

They looked at each other and braced themselves for their short sprint. Sinead did her best to bear as much of her own weight as possible. They ran to the truck, heading to the side furthest away from the entrance to the building. It was an old run-down building, with metal double doors and metal bars on the broken windows. Yolanda pulled back the dirty white tarp; there were a number of crates with various fruits and vegetables in them, leaving hardly any place to hide. She made space for the three of them, then climbed in the back, pushing the taller crates forward. She then leant over the side of the truck, and pulled Sinead into the back while Kailum gave Sinead a leg boost.

They could hear voices and the sound of someone coming towards them. Kailum looked over the side of the truck; the guy was coming back, but he was standing with his back to the truck as he finished his conversation with whoever was in the building.

"Quick!" Yolanda hissed, as she dragged Sinead into the back of the truck, with Kailum promptly following.. They ducked behind the crates and pulled the tarp over themselves. They waited for their driver to return. And he did. He jumped straight into the driver's side of the truck, started the engine, and pulled away. The three cousins sat in the back, Sinead with her head on Yolanda's lap, drifting in and out of what they hope was sleep, and not a coma.

The driver carried on his journey for a few more hours, occasionally stopping, and removing various barrels and crates from the back of the truck.

"At some point, we will have to jump out, before he sees us," Kailum said, in a low voice to Yolanda.

"Have a quick look, and check where we are now," Yolanda suggested.

Kailum scanned the section of the city within his view. "It's just derelict buildings; everything looks the same," he said, with a hint of disappointment in his voice. The driver returned and jumped back in, started up his truck and pulled away once again. This time he drove without stopping; the children didn't know how long it had been, but it was much longer than his earlier drop-offs. Kailum looked again from underneath the tarp.

"Can you see anything?" whispered Yolanda

"No buildings, it's just rocks and dust, the road looks bumpy," Kailum said, as the truck dove over a load of rocks, making Kailum bump his head on the side. The sudden jerk woke Sinead.

"Where are we?" she mumbled. "What's happening?"

"Sssh," said Yolanda, peeking out her side of the truck. "He might be finished with his deliveries; we should try to jump off now. It looks remote, so no one will notice us." The three children crawled on their hands and knees, making their way out from under the tarp, crawling pass the last couple of barrels at the front of the truck.

The three looked at each other.

"Ready?" whispered Yolanda, and the other two nodded. Together, they jumped from the truck, onto the dirt road, rolling towards the ditch. Not entirely breaking their fall as smoothly as they had hoped, but it was good enough. They watched as the truck drove on into the dusk of the evening, unaware of the stowaways that had just leaped to freedom.

CHAPTER 15

A Sand Storm

They laid in the ditch for a while; Sinead suffering the worst, after her second tumble of the day. Yolanda was happy to stretch out her aching limbs that had developed cramps after being stuck in such a small space for so long. Kailum was equally pleased to relax in peace for a short while.

"It'll be dark soon; we need to decide what to do next," Yolanda said, as she laid there, staring up at the handful of stars that pushed their way into the evening sky.

"We could stay here," Kailum suggested, as he listened to the peaceful sound of the crickets.

"We'd freeze to death," Yolanda pointed out. "We need to find shelter."

Although tired, and not in the mood to search for new accommodation, the three cousins had to hunt for some place to sleep.

"Where's Elicia?" Sinead asked suddenly, as she sat up, stunned. Looking one to another, neither Yolanda nor Kailum could remember when they had last seen Elicia.

"What? She isn't here?" Sinead had panic in her voice.

"I can't remember when I last saw her," Kailum was honest.

"She could be kidnapped!" Sinead's voice was high and filled with panic.

"She was with you, at the market, last time I saw her," Yolanda said.

"And you left her there?" Sinead shouted.

"I was busy rescuing you!" Yolanda shouted back, in defence.

"Calm down: someone might hear you," Kailum said, using hand gestures to emphasise how loud they both were.

"We have to find her," Sinead said, in a low panicked voice. "We have to go back; we can't leave her there."

"Go back?" with her right hand held firmly against her head, Yolanda could not disguise the shock in her voice. "You don't understand what we went through to escape that place."

"We can't leave a man behind," Kailum said, climbing out of the ditch.

"Welcome to reality; we aren't one of your war games," Yolanda said, annoyed.

"Kailum's right, we can't leave her behind," Sinead agreed. "If we had done what Moses and Enoch had said, we wouldn't be in this mess." Sinead couldn't help adding.

Yolanda glared at her in anger. "Are you saying it's my fault?" Her face burnt red and her fists clenched so tightly, her knuckles were white. She turned and walked back in the direction that the truck had brought them from; Sinead and Kailum walked silently behind her.

They walked quietly along the road, and although it was dark, the moon was bright, and seemed to be pouring extra light on the road. Stars twinkled by the millions in the sky, each one encouraging the children to push forward on their journey.

"I've never seen so many stars in the sky before," Kailum said, in a low voice breaking the silence. "But I've never been out this late before either."

"I think with city lights, it's harder to notice them," said Sinead glad for the conversation as the silence made the journey harder. Furthermore, she was finding it hard to ignore the pounding in her head.

They had walked for roughly an hour towards the city, when a strong wind picked up and blew dust in their eyes and faces. The children turned their backs to the wind and put their hands over their eyes and mouths.

"I think it's a sandstorm," Kailum shouted, above the howl of the wind.

"What can we do?" Yolanda shouted, now standing next to Kailum.

"I don't know," he said, putting his right hand up to protect his eyes. "Let's take cover in that ditch," he pointed to the side of the road. The ditch was just piles of sand, built up on the side of the road, and falling into a slope of rocks and dirt.

"What do you want from us?" Sinead shouted. "Why have you brought us here? Everything that's gone wrong is your fault."

Kailum and Yolanda both looked at Sinead to see which one of them she was blaming. She was not talking to either of them but was looking up, shouting at the night sky.

"It's your fault Elicia is missing! It's your fault we are in the middle of nowhere" Sinead carried on shouting.

Kailum and Yolanda looked at Sinead in shock; she wasn't joking, she was shouting at God.

"Where is Elicia?" Sinead shouted from the top of her lungs.

"Here I am," the familiar American voice said.

The three spun around to find Elicia standing in the centre of the road with a dark-haired boy. Both appeared as if from nowhere.

The others stared in disbelief.

"Where did you come from?" Yolanda said finding her voice.

Sinead ran to Elicia and hugged her, still not believing her own eyes.

"I'm so sorry I lost you," Sinead sobbed. "Are you ok? How did you get here?" endless questions flowed from Sinead as she hugged Elicia.

"Aram brought me," Elicia said calmly.

"What? Who?" Yolanda looked at the tall dark-skinned boy, with loose curly haired that fell to his shoulders. "Who are you?"

"Rabbi Enoch has sent me to bring you back to them," Aram said with a smile.

"Well, I for one have no objections to going back there," Kailum said, with relief in his voice. "So where is your car?" he asked, ready to leave straight away.

Aram stepped back from the group, and with a smile said "Here is my car." Suddenly, wings appeared from behind him. Aram glowed as his wings reached their full breadth. Sinead, Yolanda, and Kailum looked on in shock. Yolanda walked towards Aram, and cautiously, but suspiciously, stood next to him and gradually let her eyes trace their way along his back, travelling from his neck to his lower back, and back up again until she made eye contact with him. He smiled at her as his wings fluttered gently in the night breeze. Yolanda was silent. They were wings; wings attached to his back, like a bird. Yolanda, mesmerised by what stood in front of her, reached out her hand and gently stroked the right wing. Soft and smooth to the touch, they glistened in the moonlight, as if each feather was covered in thousands of tiny jewels.

"It's so cool," Elicia said, encouraging her cousins. "Kailum, you'll love it," she said, full of enthusiasm.

"What makes you think we are going with you?" Yolanda tried to cover up her embarrassment, as she realised how personal she had got with Aram.

"We've had a day where grown-ups have chased us, tried to burn us alive," Sinead added. "Now you want us to go with you; why should we trust you?"

"You trust Rabbi Enoch and Moses, don't you?" Aram smiled, un-fazed by Sinead's tone. "Do you trust an angel of God?"

"How do we know you're an angel of God?" Yolanda said, with an untrusting look in her eyes.

"Because of his wings; they glow white," Elicia answered. "And he brought me to you. Are you coming with me?" Elicia looked from one cousin to the other, letting them know she would not stay out in the middle of nowhere, so late at night, when she had somewhere safe to go.

"Did you ever think of asking God for help, instead of shouting at him?" Aram asked Sinead.

She looked at him stunned; anger surged deep inside her.

Her face felt hot as her heart rate increased. She gritted her teeth and glared at Aram, her face turning bright red.

"I don't think it is any of your business," she said, in a sharp tone. "Aren't you meant to be taking us somewhere?" she added, looking at Aram, thinking he looked familiar.

"Well, step closer and we can get ready," Aram said, unshaken by Sinead's response. He stretched out his wings, encasing the group, allowing the tips of each wing to touch the other.

"This will be great fun," Elicia said, with a big smile. "You'll think you're flying."

The children watched the dust on the road build up into a funnel around them; it looked as though they were in the centre of the eye of the storm.

They felt themselves float upwards, and then in different directions.

CHAPTER 16

Blacked Winged Beast

As they flew, Aram spotted a dark shadow from out of the corner of his eye. It flew high above, stretching out its wings as it circled the young group. Its wings sent loud clicking sounds that pierced the night air as it flew. The black-winged creature swooped and ducked through the air, moving closer to the group, sending fear to its prey while feeding its own curiosity. Its head was flat and wide, with the shape of a serpent's mouth, but instead of fangs it had two rows of razor-sharp teeth. Just under its flat wide nose it had a pointed tusk, with two more on either side of its cheeks. Its head, covered in a tough, rough animal hide, was essentially body armour. Its black body was long and sleek, covered in fish-like scales, with long black wings extending from the back of its neck, behind the armour, to its pointy serpent tail. There were over two thousand fine slender bones running through its wings; the bones rubbed against each other as the black-winged creature flew, creating a loud clicking sound that vibrated through the air, which soon became a warning sound to many of its prey.

Aram knew the beast was not looking for them out of curiosity; it was one of Lumiel's flying underdogs, searching for prey to capture and take back to its master.

Black-winged creatures normally fled at the sight of a celestial being, but Aram guessed the news of the children had spread, and there was a bounty on each of their heads. The black-winged creature, now flying close to the ground, had its sights on Aram, and intended grabbing at least one child. This outweighed its fear of the young celestial being. Diving close, the creature built up its courage to take its first strike against the group.

Aram realised he could not out-fly the creature; the weight of the four children was slowing him down, but he still had to protect his charges. With a sudden change in direction, he doubled back and landed on the ground with such force it sent a shockwave through the earth, causing the buildings in the nearby cities and towns to shake.

Aram hoped the vibration had stunned the creature and knocked it off its course, but the black-winged beast came back, brave and fierce, screaming a loud pitch screech as it prepared to fight.

Flames of fire shot from its mouth as it swooped down towards the group. Aram dodged the oncoming flames. Enfolding his wings around the children, he reached over his shoulder and pulled his bow to the front. Then he picked an arrow from his leather quiver with his left hand and rested it between the arch of the bow and the long silk bow string. He aimed his arrow, pointing it straight at the black winged beast. With absolute skill and accuracy, he pulled back on the bow, releasing the arrow from its cradle, letting it spin through the air with great speed, as it hurtled towards its target.

The arrow spun through the night air; clipping the black wing, it shattered the bones and shredded the wing. The beast howled in pain, dipping low, then, in a sharp circular motion, spun upwards towards the night sky.

Aram motioned to the children to stay low; he knew the black wing would return, with reinforcements. He passed his quiver of arrows to Kailum, as he cradled another arrow between his fingers and his bow, then he pulled back on the string, pointing into the night as he waited for the return of the black wing.

Kailum took out another arrow from the leather sack. He ran his fingers over the feathers of the arrow; they felt hard to the touch, the tip of the arrow felt sharp like a blade, and Kailum guessed the creature had suffered a serious injury from Aram's last shot.

Kailum watched Aram as he held the bow and pointed the arrow towards the sky. He turned his body in a semi-circle, preparing for another attack.

From behind, there came a loud screech as the black wing spread out its wings, beating a thunderous flap and setting off such a shuddering, it raised a dust storm. The black wing set itself on a course towards Aram and the children.

Aram spun around, aiming at his target, but the angel's aim was too far to the right. The beast shot flames from its mouth, aiming at Aram; its mission was to take out the celestial being. As Aram shot his arrow at the screeching black wing, he bent forward, allowing his body and wings to cover his charges, taking on the full force of the black wing's attack.

"I need another arrow!" he shouted to Kailum, as the smell of burnt feathers filled the air. Kailum was ready and wasted no time as he passed Aram the arrow he was holding, retrieving another straight away from the quiver. Kailum watched, as Aram prepared for the next attack. The black wing flew low, confident it had weakened the young warrior.

Aram was at the top of his class in combat training, but nothing had prepared him for this. His mission was simple; locate the lost visitors and return them to the house of Enoch and Moses. No one had prepared him for this, taking on one of Lumiel's underdogs while protecting his charges. He took a deep breath; now, he needed to keep a sharp mind and keep the children safe. He pushed to the back of his mind the painful stinging sensation on his arm and back, as black burnt feathers fell to the ground.

"Let me help you," Kailum shouted. "I can watch your back."

"It's too risky!" Aram shouted above the wild screech of the black wing. The creature turned and flew in circles above the group, trying to disorientate the young warrior. Attacking Aram from behind, the black wing hit the angel on his right leg. Pain shot from Aram's knee to his ankle, causing him to buckle in agony, but he held strong, keeping the children covered. The black wing, confident in its attack against the celestial being, showed little fear against its intended target or its charges, determined to return to his master with a prisoner, regardless of whether they were dead or alive.

The creature prepared to make one last descent on the young group, when a loud thunderous clap was heard in the heavens. Three brilliant white stallions appeared in the night sky. Mounted on each stallion were the archangels Raguel, Barchiel and Raphael. Halting in mid-flight, the black wing was distracted by the oncoming angelic army. It regained its composure then swooped towards its young target. The Archangels reached the earth with great speed; Raguel and Barchiel surrounded the young group, and Raphael charged towards the black wing, which had now been joined by four other flying creatures, known as the Pickers.

Pickers were scavenger hunters, who preyed on the injured or the dying, and were known to fight alongside the black wings. Tall creatures, reaching thirteen feet in height, with long slender necks, and a small round head with four large beady eyes, two at the front and two at the back. Their oval bodies were small and stocky, covered in coarse hair; their four long thin legs, interwoven with their wings, were covered in layers of membrane.

Raphael pulled out his flaming sword, holding it high in his right hand, with his shield in his left. The flaming sword lit up the night sky, revealing the name of YHWH on his breast plate.

Raphael charged towards two of the Pickers, swinging his sword from right to left, with an upward motion followed by a downward swoop. A strong scent of burnt feathers drifted in the night air as he advanced forward, taking out both pickers with one swift swipe of his sword.

Raguel and Barchiel remained on the ground, taking out the black wing and the other pickers, as they stood guard over Aram and the children, their flaming swords lighting up the sky, sending out fear to any other black wings or pickers who dared to join the battle.

In a short time, the battle was over. Raphael returned to Aram and ran his hand over Aram's injures. The glorious heat from the archangel's hand sent a soothing sensation over Aram's leg, running through his back, healing the burns on his body.

A scar now ran down his back where his burnt wings used to be.

"This is your war wound," Raphael told Aram, with an encouraging smile, and he sent Aram and the children back to Enoch and Moses, under the protection of Raguel and Barchiel.

CHAPTER 17

Lumiel

"Is it true, you had them within your grasp and then they eluded you?" Lumiel asked. "Come now, I'm a reasonable man; you can be honest with me," he smiled.

Sitting patiently, in the inner chamber, a tall man dressed in white, with long black hair falling loosely over his shoulders, reclined in a gold-carved chair with a high back and wide armrests. Good-naturedly, tapping the long slender fingers of his right hand on the gold-carved armrests and sending a pulsating echo throughout the room, he scratched his chin with his left hand as he thoughtfully studied his guests. Rising, he walked towards them, his dark eyes searching out their faces, sensing their fear. Why wouldn't they be terrified? They were standing in front of greatness. His tall elegant statue appeared to glide rather than walk, as he proceeded across the room and circled all three men.

"They used wicked trickery to escape us," one boldly replied.

Lumiel stood in front of the man who spoke; he was of average height, with a long scraggly beard and smelled like he had not washed in months. Grabbing the man's head with both hands, Lumiel closed his eyes, and for a few moments concentrated as he drew out images from the man's memory. Gradually, everything that had happened in the marketplace was being revealed to him through telepathy. He saw two of the children kick over the table of fish; he watched as grown men fell prey to the childish prank. He understood now why the man smelt so bad; he saw the man regain his footing and run towards the table that was covered with various types of fabrics. Through the man's own eyes, he saw a young girl, with long blonde hair, hiding under the table and the celestial being grab the child and pull her from the man's grasp. He let go of the bearded man; he understood why the man described it as evil trickery.

Lumiel moved on to the next man; without saying a word, he looked at the short skinny man, then placed his hands on the man's bald head and watched as he followed a tall dark-haired girl running towards a building. The bald man, along with two others slipped on oil as the girl took the opportunity to escape inside the building, locking the door behind her. The bald man used some oil to start a fire by the doorway, clearly trying to smoke out his victim. Then Lumiel watched as another man, tall and slim, with shoulder-length wavy brown hair, broke open a window in the next building. Both he and the bald man climbed through and headed to the roof. they jumped across to the adjacent building where the young dark-haired girl was hiding.

The tall man noticed the dangling cable thrown over the side of the building and ran to investigate. He saw the girl trying to escape. Lumiel saw their efforts in trying to haul her back up to the roof, but surprisingly she let go, and her companions, waiting below, helped her escape.

Lumiel let go of the bald man's head. Silently he looked at the third tall, slim man standing with his eyes averted towards the floor. Lumiel said nothing; they had tried, but they had also failed. He pondered on their punishment. He pursed his lips, as he looked them up and down. With a flick of his hand, he waved them away; two of his guards took them back to the cages.

Lumiel went back to his seat. Crossing his legs, he tapped his lips with his right index finger. "They let them escape. Leave them in the cages for a couple of days; it may teach them not to fail me again." Lumiel paused, looking at one of his lead soldiers. "Azazel, you think I've gone soft."

"No, my Lord," Azazel said, worried that his tone would give him away.

"Well, you may be correct, but they may come in handy at a later time, and after all, they are like loyal dogs," Lumiel said, and Azazel laughed in agreement.

"The children have a celestial guarding them; we need them found before they make their way back to the house of the prophets," Lumiel said. "Send out the grey-dacs to find them." Lumiel looked at Azazel, "I want the children alive."

The greydacs were Lumiel's favourites of all his beasts. He knew their appearance alone put fear in mankind. They flew with little grace but were by far the strongest of all the hybrid beasts. Lumiel treated them as his favourite pets, and they, in turn, were loyal to their master.

Lumiel sat silently for a moment, then asked Azazel to summon one of the soldiers; he had a quest for him.

Rahan entered with his head bowed and eyes lowered; he waited for his master's permission for him to approach.

"Rahan, come, I have a quest for you," Lumiel sounded even-tempered.

"My Lord," Rahan said, keeping his eyes lowered. "I am here to serve you."

"I want you to travel in the shadows, and follow the human children, distract them from their true purpose." Lumiel paused, then said, "I expect your war with Aram will not be a hindrance to your mission. How you choose to do it is entirely up to you. Go, and travel in the shadows, but travel with care."

Rahan bowed his head as he left the room, to return to his quarters and prepare for his mission.

Lumiel smiled to himself; young humans sent at this time, how intriguing. Then, looking up to the heavens, a dark glint crossed his eyes. "What are you planning, oh mighty one?" He then got up from his seat and walked across the room. Going through a door on the left, he climbed the stairs leading to the upper room. Making his way to the far side of the temple, he stood on the balcony overlooking the city. Looking up into the night sky, the stars twinkled, and the moon shone brightly as if smiling on the earth. Lumiel paused as he viewed his kingdom, breathing in the warm evening air. This was his time; this was his kingdom, and whatever roamed the lands were his subjects, even if they somehow had travelled across time itself. He smiled to himself; he had successfully confused the minds of human adults, so children would be like putty in his hands.

"I may only get to win the little battle, but I promise you this," he hissed, looking up at the night sky, "I will take as many as I can with me. They are simple human fools. They are gullible, and I have them right where I want them. Right in the palm of my hand."

Across the city, a voice was heard, a call out to prayer. Lumiel's countenance grew dark, he drew a deep breath and allowed his wings to expand to full size, sending out a stench of burnt feathers as his black wings had thrown a dark shadow over the streets below. His scarred face and burnt limbs pushed through the surface of the artificial physique that he proudly paraded among his subjects, as his anger revealed his true form.

"Your time is short, dear prophets," he said, in an angry voice. "When I take you out, I will throw the biggest party this world has ever seen, mark my words, oh favoured one." He then turned and headed back inside, with anger raging through his veins.

CHAPTER 18

The Painted Window

In a short time, they were all back in the room, the same room where their adventure had first started, with its low seats, the mosaic tiled walls, and multi-coloured stained glass windows.

Moses and Enoch were sitting at the table when the children re-appeared with Aram. As he pulled his wings back, Elicia ran to Enoch and hugged him, she then hugged Moses.

"I'm so glad to be back," she whispered in Moses' ear.

"I'm glad you're safe, both you and your cousins," Moses said hugging her and grateful she was safe.

Enoch looked at the other three children, who looked tired and hungry after their adventure.

"Come and eat," he said gesturing with his hand for them to take a seat at the table. "You must be very hungry."

"Yes, I'm starving," said Kailum. "We haven't eaten since yesterday".

They all sat around the table and started to eat;, the food was hot and tasty.

"So, did you find what you were looking for outside?" Moses asked very casually, interested in what the children thought of the outside world.

"It was very scary," Elicia said, picking up a piece of bread to eat.

Moses and Enoch looked silently at the children, waiting for them to choose their own time to share what had happened. Kailum didn't say anything; he was so hungry he felt he had not eaten for a week, and not just a day. Yolanda stared at the food on her plate, occasionally picking at a piece of chicken, but feeling guilty, she avoided any eye contact.

Sinead didn't look herself; she looked pale and drained. Aram came with a little basin of warm water and a cloth to wipe the blood from Sinead's head. She sat on the far end of the seat, away from the table, while Aram gently patted the warm, damp cloth against her head.

"Sinead, you don't look well," Enoch said. "Are you ok?"

"She bumped her head when she fell off a burning building," Kailum took a short break from eating to inform Enoch and Moses of Sinead's accident.

"She fell off a building?" Elicia gasped.

"Well, not completely. She was three-quarters of the way down when she had to let go of the cable she was using as a climbing rope," Kailum informed them.

Enoch got up and walked over to Sinead, who was now lying down and resting her head on a cushion. He put his hand on her head and started to say some words, speaking in a language that the children didn't understand. Moses joined him, sitting near Sinead and putting his hand on her shoulder as he joined in with the prayer.

"Rest now," Moses said as they finished praying. "You will feel better when you have had a good sleep." Sinead closed her eyes and gradually drifted off to sleep.

The other children continued eating their food.

"So," Moses said, deciding he had waited long enough. "Who is going to tell us what happened?"

"We went to a market," Elicia started to tell the story. "But the adults there were not very nice."

"I think they hate kids," Kailum added.

"Why do you think that?" Enoch asked.

"Well, when they saw us, they started shouting, then they chased us," Kailum said, sitting back, resting his hands on his satisfied tummy.

"I hid under a table with Sinead," Elicia said. "Then, when Sinead told me to follow her, I tried, but some man with dirty smelly feet blocked my way and I couldn't follow her."

"That must have been quite scary," Moses was sympathetic.

"Yeah, it was," Elicia said, and then turning to Kailum, "How did you guys get away, and why did Sinead fall off a building?"

Kailum explained how both he and Yolanda tripped up some angry men by knocking over a table full of fish and then escaped up a back street. Sinead, not being so lucky in her escape route from the market, had got trapped in a building. He told the story with great enthusiasm, how Sinead had climbed down the side of the building and had to let go of the rope when she was only three-quarters of the ways down.

"That's how she hurt her head," Kailum said, using hand gestures as he explained how both he and Yolanda had helped Sinead escape in the back of a truck and had fled the city, and how the driver hadn't known they were in the back of his truck.

"That was quite a scary adventure," Enoch said, when Kailum had finished his story. "Yolanda, you're silent, are you ok? He asked.

"Yes," she whispered, "I don't understand why the adults hate us so much."

"We are living in a very different time to you," Moses explained. "In these times we have no children. The adults are confused and scared, because they saw their own children disappear before their eyes." He looked at the eager little faces listening to him. "So, when they saw you it must have confused and frightened them. Others may have wanted to hand you over to their new leader."

"That is why we did not want you to leave the house and go outside; it is too dangerous for you," Enoch added.

"I'm sorry; it was my idea to leave," Yolanda said, still feeling guilty.

"It's ok, God has brought you back safely; promise not to go outside again," Enoch said in a very concerned voice.

"We promise," Elicia said, while Yolanda and Kailum nodded in agreement.

"But why were you arguing with the people outside your window?" Yolanda found the courage to ask.

"You went upstairs?" Moses said in surprise.

"Yes," Yolanda looked embarrassed. "I'm sorry. But why were you arguing?"

"We were trying to explain to the people that they need to change their lives and turn back to God," Enoch explained. "Some disagreed with us."

"A lot of bad things are happening in this time; people no longer fear God. Some are in pain and blame

The Lord, and others have decided to follow Lumiel and do the evil things that he asks of them," Moses explained to the young group.

"Why did God bring us to the future, especially if he has taken the children already?" Sinead asked, as she sat up, feeling refreshed from her sleep.

"Do you have any thoughts as to why he may have brought you to this time?" Moses asked her.

Sinead never liked it when people answered her questions with a question.

"I don't know; maybe because I'm angry with him, but I understand how it hurt him too." She said. "What about the others? They don't feel the same as I do."

Moses looked at the other three, and smiled, "do you children see The Lord as your friend?" he asked.

"I do now, because he sent Aram to rescue me," Elicia said. "Now I feel I can ask him anything. Before, I was saying and doing things because the grown-ups told me to, not because I wanted to do them myself," she said.

"We all do that," Yolanda said. "We go to church because our parents tell us, and we go to school because it's expected of us; not that we want to."

"I like school, and I don't mind going," Elicia responded.

"I think you're the only one that likes school," Kailum piped in. "I'd rather be at home than at school, any day of the week."

"It still doesn't explain why we're here," Sinead sounded a little annoyed as the conversation changed course.

"Well, the grown-ups here haven't been that nice to us," Yolanda said looking at Sinead. "The only two people that have looked after us are the two people that pray."

"They are holy people, they are meant to be nice to us," Sinead responded, a little too quickly, then looked at Enoch and Moses with a guilty look.

"It's ok, my child, you can say what's on your mind," Enoch said, smiling.

"Sorry, I didn't mean to be rude," she said meekly. "I miss my gran and I'm worried about her," Sinead said. "I want to go home."

"I'm sure you will return to your own time very soon," Moses tried to encourage the little group. "But when you leave here, what will you take with you when you return home?" He asked, looking at the young faces.

"That grown-ups in the future aren't very nice," Kailum said, knowing his response was a bit weak.

"Are all the adults in your time very nice?" asked Enoch.

"No," Kailum said.

Enoch smiled at his honesty,

"You are standing at a crossroads in your young lives; you need to make a choice for yourselves," Moses said. "To decide if you want to take the road that is good and walk down that road, or if you want to take the other road," he said.

"You mean take the other road that might have us end up like the people in the market?" Yolanda said, a bit shocked. "I don't want to be like them."

"Or me either," Kailum added.

"Everything my gran says is true," Sinead looked thoughtful. "I want to be a good, nice person. I want to live how The Lord would want me to, but I find it hard to get past losing my parents."

Enoch looked at the children; now was time for them to have a better understanding of life and death. This was the time to share God's word with them. This was the time they would understand.

"The word of God tells us," Enoch started, as he looked at the young group. "My friends, we want you to understand how it will be for those followers who have already died. Then you won't grieve over them like people who don't have any hope. We believe Jesus died and was raised to life. We also believe that when God brings Jesus back again, he will bring with him all who had faith in Jesus before they died. Our Lord Jesus told us that when he comes, we won't go up to meet him ahead of his followers who have already died.

"With a loud command and with the shout of the chief angel, and a blast of God's trumpet, the Lord will return from Heaven. Then those who had faith in Christ, before they died, will be raised to life. Next, all of us who are still alive will be taken up into the clouds, together with them, to meet the Lord in the sky. From that time on, we will all be with the Lord forever."

"Here, let me show you," said Enoch, as he got up and walked towards the great hall. He turned towards the children and motioned to them to follow him. Looking at the beautiful stained-glass windows, he pointed to the striking images on all three windows. "What do you see, children?" he asked, as they slowly gathered around him, like students gathering around their teacher as he showed them an experiment.

"Paintings of people," Yolanda was casual, the images were obvious.

"It's telling a story," Elicia added, "Just like the ones in the church at home," she said, confident in her response.

"Really?" Kailum scratched his head, slightly thrown by Elicia's remark.

"In church, they have all the saints, the holy family, and the angels," Sinead added, helping her cousin.

"Can't say I've ever really paid any attention," Kailum confessed. "I thought it was a bunch of paintings just to make the place look exciting."

"It's church, I don't think it's meant to be exciting," Yolanda said, wondering what was so exciting about this window painting.

"Well," Enoch said, moving forward and pointing to the top of the middle window. "Here you can see a bright yellow glow; if you look close enough you can see something move."

"The sun?" Kailum said, slightly curling up his top lip, with a hint of doubt in his voice.

"Not quite the sun, but if you look deep inside, there is something else," Enoch pointed into the warm yellow glow.

"It looks like someone is in there," Elicia said. "I think I can see a man."

"Oh yeah, I think I can see it now," Kailum said, with his head tilted to one side as he squinted his eyes.

"The Lord returning for his people," Enoch explained. "But he remains in the clouds, as the Angels blow the trumpets."

To the left, just below the Angels, it looked like people were sleeping, and then they floated upwards, toward the bright yellow glow. Elicia looked a little closer, "I think they're smiling."

"Yes, they are," said Moses, moving over to Elicia as he pointed to the wingless floating bodies, dressed in long white robes. "They are those that have died, and they have been, well, sleeping," he explained to the eight-year-old and her cousins.

"They have been woken by the sounds of the trumpets and will go to meet The Lord. That's when the Bible says, 'the dead in Christ will rise first'" Enoch explained.

"So, who are they, down there?" Yolanda pointed to the bottom right of the third window.

"They are all the people still living on the earth, followers of Christ; when the last trumpet is blown, they will be carried up to the clouds to meet The Lord."

"So, they are the people that will just disappear off the earth," Kailum said, still quite intrigued by the whole disappearing thing and secretly hoping he would be one of them.

"You see, there is nothing wrong with grieving the loss of a family member, but it is important to remember to have faith and know that one day we will see them again when we go to be with The Lord. Our time on earth is limited, but we are born to spend eternity with God." Enoch explained to Sinead, as she examined the painted glass window, almost expecting to see her parents dressed in white robes.

"You need to share this message with your friends, and others, when you go back to your time," Moses said, "before it's forgotten, and people have become like those in the market. It's getting late; I think you should turn in for the night and get some sleep," he added.

Moses directed the children back to the main living room, to settle down for an early night, then he and

Enoch went upstairs to their own rooms. The children lay on the long seat and talked for a little while about what they had just seen. Gradually, they drifted off to sleep.

With a loud crash, glass shattered on the floor of the large hallway; the sound of howling cut its way through the home of Enoch and Moses. Proceeding across the great hallway, it made its way to the room where the children lay sleeping. It was pitch dark. Sinead sat up, listening to the familiar sound, unsure if she was awake, or once again caught up in her dreaded nightmare. The nightmare that refused to leave, and consciously haunted her sleep. The crisp night air cut through the room, sending a shudder down her spine.

CHAPTER 19
Uninvited Visitors

"What's going on?" Yolanda whispered in the darkness.

"I don't know," Sinead whispered back, but what she was certain of was that this was not a nightmare, and she was not asleep. Something moved by her feet, knocking her blanket to the floor. Sinead sat frozen, not daring to move. The hair on the back of her neck and arms stood up, as something rustled by her feet, making its way over her legs.

"I'm scared," Elicia said in a low voice, as she crawled across the top of the seat, feeling her way towards Sinead.

"Stay, I'll look for something to protect us," Kailum said, as he jumped up and headed across the room, working his way along the wall towards a storage cupboard at the other end of the room.

Elicia hugged Sinead as they sat on the seats together. Yolanda pulled the covers closer to her. The room was freezing, and the relentless howling sent a thunderous tremor through the darkness. The door flung open; the girls screamed in fright. Kailum froze in shock, in mid-journey across the room.

A tall figure stood in the door, dressed in a long robe with shoulder-length hair.

"Come immediately to the praying room." Moses' voice was urgent as he signaled to the kids to follow him into the hallway.

The girls jumped up from their seats and ran to him; he pointed them towards the stairs and turned to look for Kailum. Kailum had made his way to the cupboard and was now going through the armour that was a carefully laid out in the armour room.

The flying beasts were no longer a nightmare; they were real. They swooped down and surrounded the building where Enoch and Moses lived. Sinead was no longer alone in her attempt to escape. She was now with Enoch, Moses and her cousins.

Kailum carried on with his mission, looking for a sword to fight with. He pulled out a variety of weapons from a cupboard.

"Seriously," Yolanda said as she watched him. "It's not time to play the action hero; this is real."

Kailum ignored her and continued to hunt for something suitable. He needed to protect his cousins; after all, they were girls, and they needed protecting.

Enoch stood on the balcony. His voice boomed as he shouted, the children unsure if he was shouting at the beast or calling out to God for protection. He raised his hands upwards towards the heavens, as dark clouds raced across the sky, followed by the roar of thunder, Enoch carried on shouting at the top of his voice, undeterred by the sound of glass crashing onto the floor in the great hallway.

The flying beasts had long outstretched wings: grey in colour, with red flames running through them. Their red-scaled heads bellowed out from either side, as the strange looking creatures breathed through their flat open nostrils. With the eyes of a snake, and five sharp pointed horns running across the top of their heads, the creatures had hard-rough pointed scale-like plates running down the length of their spines, leading to long slender tails. They were ugly, but prideful.

They swooped around the building, avoiding the balcony that Enoch stood on.

The beasts only appeared to be interested in the children; they flew past the windows, their eyes searching, hoping to capture their intended prey.

Moses told the children to go upstairs and hide in the smaller room, called the praying room. This room the beasts did not dare to enter. He ushered the three girls toward the stairs and turned around to find Kailum hunting for a weapon. He called to Kailum to grab the sword and hurry.

"We need more than a sword!" Kalum shouted back, as he picked up a bow and a quiver of arrows and flung them over his shoulders.

Moses ran to help him as he ran across the main hall, to the armour cupboard.

Elicia stood by the door, shouting to Kailum, "Hurry, we need to hide!"

Just then, there was a large crash of more breaking glass in the large hallway. Sinead put her hands in front of her eyes to protect them from the shards of glass that fell around her. She looked towards the doorway of the room where they had just been sleeping, but she couldn't see Elicia. Her little cousin had disappeared, caught by one of the beasts, clutched in its large claws. The little girl screamed and shouted for help.

Sinead screamed at the beast, "Let her go you big ugly coward!" the beast turned and snarled at her, but Sinead, who felt afraid at first, was now thinking she had to forget her own fears and rescue her little cousin.

Moses was on the other side of the hallway by the main room with Kalum. He slid the sword across the floor to Sinead; she needed something to defend herself with. Kalum, standing at the opposite side to Sinead, shot an arrow at the beast. He discovered that shooting real arrows was not the same as shooting targets on his Xbox game. This was real, and the bow was heavy.

Moses called to Elicia, "Do not be afraid, my child, they feed off fear." Elicia wriggled and screamed. A second beast flew through the broken window.

Aram joined Kailum and Moses and shot his own arrows at the beasts. "These are Lumiel's big dogs; he calls them grey-dacs. It won't be as easy to fight them off, not like the black wings or the pickers," Aram explained to Kailum as he shot his arrow at the beast.

"Who is Lumiel?" Kailum asked, as he positioned himself and shot his arrows at the beast's wing, but all that did was bruise it. The beast turned and snarled at him, with hot air flaring through its nostrils. Aram shot another arrow towards the beast, to distract it away from Kailum.

"Lumiel is the evil dictator of our time," Moses explained. "He has lied and deceived so many and taken control of the Holy Temple. Those who refuse to worship him are put to death," he explained as he stood in front of Kailum, protecting the young boy from the grey-dacs.

"No wonder people are scared or angry; it's practically the dark ages," Kailum said, as he continued to aim and shoot his arrows, from behind Moses.

Yolanda watched from the side of the staircase and cried, "Help her, someone, help her!"

Sinead swung the sword as best as she could, but now they had two beasts to fight.

Enoch ran to the top of the stairs and saw the chaos. "They have come for the children," he cried. "They're the only four children on the earth, and they want them."

"You can't have me, you can never have me!" Elicia screamed at the beast, that had her clasped in its claws. She fought, kicked and punched the beast with as much strength she could muster up.

"My daddy will kill you!" she shouted. "He loves me, and he will find you and kill you." The beast looked at Elicia as it held her in its claws, and with a deep guttural sound, and showing all its broken teeth, it snarled at her. Its breath smelt of a thousand dead animals, as the polluted stench covered the room. Elicia's long blonde hair blew wildly over her face, as she tried to hold her breath, to avoid a lungful of the stench from the beast's brutal rotten breath.

The other beast swooped down towards Sinead. She swung her sword towards him, but he was swift, grabbing the sword with one claw and Sinead with the other.

Aram shot arrows at the second beast, aiming at its right eye, while the beast held on to a struggling Sinead in its left claw. Aram grazed it above its scaly brow. The beast swung around, preparing to breathe fire at the celestial being, when Enoch shouted at both beasts. "Let the children go!" the beasts paused in their battle for a moment, and just for a second, they both looked as if they were smiling at the old man, both knowing Enoch or Moses dare not attack them, as they had two of the children in their grasp, and prophets would not risk killing the children.

Enoch and Moses both stood in front of Yolanda and Kalum, protecting them from the grey-dacs and not allowing the intruders to get their claws on either child.

A third beast made its way through the broken window, while a fourth smashed its way through another.

Aram carried on shooting his arrows at the grey-dacs. Stretching out his wings, he flew eye level towards his target; if they couldn't see, it would be harder for them to gauge the direction of the next attack. The third beast, clawing its way through the broken window, spread its wings to their full extent, and with a downwards swoop, hit the celestial being, sending Aram crashing to the floor. Aram regained his footing quickly, so not to allow the beast to overpower him. The beast prepared for another descent on the young Angel; with its wings outstretched, it planned to swoop again. Kailum returned from the armour cupboard with another sword, and with one swing slid the sword across the floor into Aram's reach. The young Angel swiftly grabbed the gold sword that had stopped just by his feet. Aram, with one graceful sweep, swung the sword at the descending beast, cutting through the right wing. The beast howled in pain as it gathered itself up and prepared for another attack, while the fourth tried to crash its way through the window.

Enoch opened his mouth, as if to shout at the third beast, but there were no words. A silent vibration shook the room; pictures and ornaments on the walls came crashing down from the tremor that sent a shock wave through the house. Moses followed, copying Enoch and projected the silent vibration towards the fourth beast as it crashed its way through the window. Flames burst out of the mouths of both men. The beasts retreated, trying to escape the power behind the glorious flames, which both men freely controlled. One of the beast's eyes melted like wax as it was hit by the flames from Enoch's mouth. The other was hit by Moses on the side of the face, leaving it scarred, and burning the top of its wing. Both recoiled, and with great determination, they escaped through the open window.

Sinead, hearing Elicia shout that her daddy loved her, remembered what Enoch had told them about the power of the love of Jesus. She looked straight into the eye of the beast which had her clutched in its claw and drawn her up to its eye level.

"You can't have me!" she shouted at it, "Because I belong to Jesus; he loves me." Sinead, looking to Elicia, said, "Remember, Elicia, Jesus died for us because he loves us. Remember what Enoch and Moses taught us."

Both beasts howled together, as if something had pierced deep into their flesh causing them great pain.

Elicia and Sinead shouted together, "We belong to Jesus, he loves us! He loves us!" The more they shouted, the louder the beasts howled.

Time appeared to slow down, everything moving in slow motion. The beasts let go their grip on the children. Both girls were free, falling towards the ground. The creatures howled and screamed in pain. Enoch and Moses ran towards Sinead and Elicia, with their arms outstretched, catching each girl in their arms. Then swinging around, they positioned their backs to the beasts, protecting the girls. The beasts exploded from the inside out. Their blood and guts sprayed across the walls and floors of the great hallway. For a moment everything was silent and still.

A voice broke the silence, "Ah, gross." Enoch and Moses looked towards the armour cupboard and saw Kailum covered in yellow gunk.

"Why didn't you hide?" Moses asked.

"What, and miss the greatest game of the century?" Kailum said. "My Xbox doesn't have the games with graphics effects like this," he said, as he wiped yellow gunk from his head.

Everyone laughed; Kailum looked a funny sight, but he had lightened the mood after a very intense battle.

CHAPTER 20
The Gift

"That was scary," Elicia said, as her body shook with shock.

"Come and sit down," Enoch said ushering her back into the room towards the seats.

"Aram, can you make everyone sweet tea please?" he kindly instructed the young Angel who stood next to Kailum.

"Yes, Rabbi," Aram responded and went to the kitchen.

Sinead looked pale as she sat down next to her cousins.

"Are you ok?" Kailum asked, looking at his cousin, who now was as white as a ghost.

"Did you bump your head again?" Yolanda asked sounding concerned.

"No, I'm fine," Sinead responded, feeling self-conscious as she realised everyone's eyes were on her.

Aram returned from the kitchen with cups of hot tea sitting on a tray, with a sugar bowl filled with sugar lumps, and a jug of milk. He placed the tray on the table and looked at Sinead.

"You look as if you have seen a ghost," he said

"I think I have seen a ghost," was Sinead's response "I've seen my nightmare appear before my eyes." She looked at the other faces around the table, then turning to Enoch and Moses, "I have been having these nightmares for months."

Sinead explained her dream to both men while her cousins sat silently sipping sweet tea.

"I don't understand; what does it mean?" She asked them.

"Sounds like it could be your gift developing," Enoch said.

"A gift! How could a nightmare be a gift?" Yolanda said in disbelief.

"God has given each one of us gifts. Sinead may have the gift of prophecy, predicting events before they happen. It is a gift where you receive messages from God. It can be anything, from warnings to guidance, to kind words in tough times."

"Wow, you can see into the future that's so cool!" Kailum said excitedly. "I hope I have something cool like that."

"Well, it's a message from God, not looking into the future." Moses reiterated, making sure what he was saying was not misinterpreted. Tapping Kailum on the back he said, "I'm sure in time you will receive your gift. Everyone will receive their gifts," he emphasised as he looked to Yolanda and Elicia.

"What am I supposed to do with it?" Sinead looked confused.

"You will help others," Enoch explained, "But first you will need to learn and understand it."

"How?" asked Yolanda

"God will make a way. He will put the right people beside you to teach you and help you." Enoch answered, but he could tell that Yolanda was not convinced. "It is one reason you are here, to discover these gifts, discover who you are."

"We fell through some type of time loop, to find out we can see into the future?" Yolanda wasn't buying it.

"That, and other things you have learned while you were here," Moses said. "Things you are not being taught in your time. Things that grown-ups have decided not to teach in your time anymore," Moses explained, in a serious tone.

"How did you know?" Kailum asked in surprise.

"The Lord showed us that in your time people have stopped believing and teaching their children regarding their faith in him. They have stopped prayers in school, and his name has become a swear word, instead of being praised for what he has done for mankind." Moses looked to Elicia. "Some parents are still doing their best to make sure their children know about God and the truth of salvation. But many are being deprived of this precious information. Many will grow up not knowing the truth and they will one day become like the adults you saw here in the market, lost and afraid because they did not grow up knowing the truth."

He looked around at the silent eager faces. "That is why you are here at this time to see what happens and teach others about it. Children talk to children and they listen to each other. Time is short, and this message needs to be shared. You must share with other children on the earth, so they, too, make wise decisions for themselves."

"Don't worry, God will always give you the help you need, and Aram has been assigned to be your guide in this important quest. Now, we must get you ready to go back home," Enoch said, encouraging the young group.

Elicia sat closer to Enoch and hugged him. "Will we ever see you again?"

"Yes, we will meet again one day," Enoch smiled.

"I'm so glad I got to come here and meet you both," Elicia said, as she hugged Enoch and then walked over to Moses and hugged him.

The group got up from the table and each hugged the two men as they said their goodbyes, and then stood in the centre of the room. Aram once again encased the children within his wings.

"Remember to return them back to the exact time they were in," Moses instructed Aram.

Aram nodded, and within a blink of an eye, they had left the room. Each child returning to their own home in their own time, in front of their own computer. But one thing was different: they were each wearing a white, roped chain around their necks and hanging from the chain was a small clear stone. A reminder of their trip and where they had been.

The End

Message from the Author

Dear Reader

Thank you so much for purchasing my book. I hope you enjoyed reading it. Please leave a review on whatever site you used to by the book from.

Sinead, Yolanda, Kailum and Elicia adventures continues in **Shadow Jumper Book 2 "Land of the Giants"**

To be notified when it releases follow the link below

https://forms.gle/i8uFdESjffNAVi5U8